STAR WARS™

JOIN THE RESISTANCE

WRITTEN BY

BEN ACKER & BEN BLACKER

ILLUSTRATED BY

ANNIE WU

DisNEY

LUCASFILM
PRESS

LOS ANGELES · NEW YORK

Acker & Blacker dedicate this book to their parents—Larry and Donna Acker and Richard & Karen Blacker—for their love, for their support, and for bringing them to see the original trilogy in the theater and buying them so many action figures.

CHAPTER
01

"ARE YOU READY for an adventure?"

Mattis looked up from the viewport where he was watching Durkteel, his home, the only planet he'd ever known, disappear into the distance. He blinked back the lingering wink of the stars and let the compartment of the ship come into focus. He found himself face to face with a short Rodian who seemed to be made of limbs and fingers.

"Are you ready for an adventure?" the skinny Rodian asked again. He spoke like his words were funneled out of his nose, because they were.

Mattis smiled. It was a question he had wanted to hear his whole life. He *was* ready.

"I'm Klimo!" the Rodian told him, squeezing in on the bench beside Mattis and annoying a Zeltron girl who was sitting near enough that she slid away from them. "I'm Klimo," he said loudly at her. "We'll all be friends soon!"

Mattis wasn't so sure. That Zeltron girl didn't seem to like Klimo very much. Mattis hoped that the other new recruits wouldn't find the Rodian annoying. You only joined the Resistance once. You didn't want to get off on the wrong foot.

Mattis knew that Klimo was just excited. So was Mattis. So was everyone on the transport. Mattis was taking in every detail, so he could see others fidgeting in their seats. A Wookiee's leg bounced up and down. A Saurin tapped a finger against the wall as if he was ticking off the seconds in transit. Everyone was excited and nervous and full of wonder and panic. Even that Zeltron girl, who was playing it off like she joined the Resistance all the time, was forcing herself to breathe evenly, Mattis was sure.

Mattis stuck out his hand toward Klimo, who grabbed it in his green fingers and put Mattis's digits through a complex dance that was supposed to be a friendly handshake. Klimo released

Mattis's hand after tugging on his pointer finger and blowing wetly through his funnel of a snout.

Mattis laughed. "I'm Mattis," he said. "Mattis Banz."

"I'm Klimo!" Klimo shouted, unable to contain himself. He leaped from the bench again and dashed back and forth through the compartment.

"You should sit down," Mattis said, loud enough to get credit for trying. "We'll get to the base soon enough." Klimo wasn't listening. He was pestering the nervous-kneed Wookiee, a terrible idea. Mattis hoped the others appreciated his effort to calm the Rodian. His leadership. *Already.* After all, Mattis knew it was only a matter of time before he was a hero of the Resistance.

Mattis had been ready for an adventure for as long as he could remember. From the first time he heard the stories about the scrappy and courageous Rebellion overthrowing the dark and giant Empire, Mattis knew his place in the universe was as a galactic champion like Luke Skywalker or Leia Organa or even Admiral Ackbar. Those names loomed large for Mattis, as if they'd been carved into fifty-meter-tall stone tablets. Hearing their stories from the older kids at the orphan farm in Lund Gourley as they tilled the hemmel fields or drift-shuttled to the Phirmist temple had stirred something in Mattis. He knew there was no more Empire to fight, but the tales made Mattis want to be a good person, a *great* person, like his heroes. He would always try to do the right thing. He would stand up for those who couldn't stand up for themselves.

So Mattis searched around every corner for adventure. He honed his heroic instincts and acted heroic whenever he could, which was mostly in little ways. Marn, the orphan mistress, ensured that the orphans had water and food, sent them to the hemmel fields, and being an old Phirmist herself, sent them to the temple often. She wasn't cruel, but she wasn't quite kind. She was old, and she was only one person with tasks enough to keep three busy. When the smaller children were left with scraps, Mattis heroically shared his rations. When they couldn't lug their hemmel load to the splitter, Mattis heroically dragged it across the fields for them. When the older kids teased the younger orphans, Mattis heroically intervened.

Mattis didn't know it at the time, but the

Resistance had noticed his acts. Unfortunately, a Saurin teenager named Fikk took notice of Mattis, too, on the drift shuttle to Lund Gourley center one day. Like most Saurins, Fikk wasn't tall but had a body like a tree trunk. He could lift more hemmel bales than any of the other kids. Mattis had lived among Saurins on and off for years. He knew their jagged teeth and knobby reptilian heads, their dark eyes, and their horrible hiss didn't mean they were nastier or nicer than any other species. Fikk, though, was nasty.

"You been at the farm a long time," Fikk said to Mattis that day on the drift shuttle.

It wasn't a question. It felt like an insult or even a challenge, but Mattis couldn't figure out why. So he just said, "Yeah, I have," and went back to playing Rocks and Sand with one of the little kids.

That wasn't enough for Fikk. He crawled out of his seat and sidled down the aisle toward Mattis. His thick tongue touched his scaly lips.

"Tchock told me you want to fly," Fikk said, motioning with his head to the Cerean boy. Tchock dropped his conical head into his hands.

"I want to be a pilot," Mattis said. It was true, and it wasn't a secret. Mattis practiced all the time on the roto-cropper, and he'd gotten pretty good at it. The cropper couldn't get more than a few meters off the ground, but it was just like flying, only lower. Mattis loved everything about flying. From the time he was young, Mattis had read whatever he could about the birds of the galaxy and could answer pretty much any question about them. In his dreams, he flew every ship he'd ever seen.

Fikk leaned over Mattis's seat. "If you want to fly, I'll make you fly."

"I'm doing okay, thanks." Mattis laughed, hoping to make it all friendly.

"As soon as this drift stopsss, I think I'll help you fly, yeah." Fikk nodded, agreeing with himself, and then stalked back to his own seat.

Mattis spent the remainder of the drift ride in a panic. Sweat trickled down the side of his head. Burm, the kid beside him, offered, "Maybe he really does want to show you how to fly." But Fikk was a mean kid, and there was no way he had a ship.

Mattis waited as long as he could after all the others exited the drift. Something would surely attract Fikk's attention, averting the fight, and what was more heroic than ending a fight without a single blow? When he finally emerged, Mattis saw that Fikk had found a way to pass the time. He was holding up one of the youngest kids by the arm and using the kid's dangling feet to write bad words in the dirt. Mattis wasn't sure of the kid's name—Beekha? Beckgam? He was new to the orphanage, a refugee from someplace on the Outer Rim. Wherever he was from, that wasn't what he was for!

"Put him down!" Mattis shouted at Fikk.

Mattis realized he was acting heroically without even trying. He was pleased with himself even as Fikk smiled, showing his sharp teeth, and dropped the kid. Beckgam was his name, Mattis remembered.

"Get out of here, Beckgam," Mattis said. "Join the others." The kid hurried away and ran behind Tchock.

"Ready to fly?" Fikk asked, taking a step forward. Mattis took a step backward, wishing the drift shuttle driver would look up from her controls and intervene.

"If you're not, I can give Beckgam another lesssssson. Come back here, Beckgam," he called.

Mattis tried to give the boy a look that kept him where he was and it worked! Mattis turned back to face Fikk. He probably couldn't handle himself against the Saurin—Fikk was bigger and stronger, not to mention eager for a confrontation—but as long as the little kids were safe from the bully, Mattis wasn't worried. Well, he was a little worried. But being worried about yourself is different from being worried about others.

"I don't want to fly," Mattis said as Fikk took another step toward him.

"That's not what Tchock ssssaid."

Tchock, at a safe distance, dropped his head in his hands again.

"That's not what everyone saysss. You want to fly, Mattisss, ssso fly!" With that, Fikk hunched over and ran toward Mattis. Mattis was excited to learn whether he knew how to fight and was quickly disappointed to learn that he did not. The Saurin grabbed Mattis around the middle, knocking the wind out of him. He hoisted Mattis over his shoulder. Mattis kicked at the air and managed to wrap an arm around Fikk's face. The scales were warm, which Mattis didn't expect.

Fikk laughed. It sounded like a sharp cough. Mattis didn't think any of it was funny. He slapped his palm hard against Fikk's face, and Fikk laughed harder and sharper.

"You're flying, big boy!" Fikk teased.

Mattis wriggled off Fikk's shoulder and hung upside down against Fikk's back.

He screamed for Fikk to stop, and he didn't like the way it sounded. He felt his face turn red with exertion and embarrassment and from being upside down.

"Stop sssqueaking, big boy! You're a pilot now!" Fikk hissed. "How are the Gs treating you?" Mattis kicked and thrashed and pounded at Fikk. All he got for his effort was that sharp cough-laugh again. He felt tears rise in his eyes. He blinked them back.

"I hear you whimpering back there. What are you doing, baby? You're crying, aren't you?" Fikk hoisted Mattis up so they were face to face.

Mattis forced a smile, but it came out mean, meaner than Fikk's hot breath in his face.

"I know what you want," Mattis told him. "You can't produce tears of your own, so you want to see mine. Tough sand, *big boy*."

They stared at each other. They might have stared at each other for millennia if the drift driver hadn't made a racket descending the shuttle's steps. Fikk put Mattis back on his feet but kept an arm around him, a clawed hand tight on his shoulder.

"You boys all right?" the driver asked. Mattis had forgotten she was still there.

"Jusssst playing," Fikk said. His sunken black eyes revealed nothing.

The drift driver was a Skup with stooped shoulders, long arms, a bulbous stomach, and close-set eyes that peered through air-baked hair. She gave Mattis a look that asked, *Is this kid lying to me?*

Mattis knew that Marn was of a mind that if a kid was old enough (which Fikk was) and a troublemaker (which Fikk was), they'd be sent to make trouble somewhere the professionals plied that same trade: Lund Berlo. Even for a Saurin, the dominant species there, that was a dangerous prospect.

Mattis shook his head and said, "We're just having fun."

The drift driver nodded and fixed her face with a loose smile that might have been a grimace. "Don't have so much fun," she said. "Not near my barge."

Fikk nodded, and Mattis said okay. Fikk gave him a look that Mattis hoped indicated a new respect between them, and Mattis gave him one back. The drift driver shooed them away, and making a clever choice for once in his life, Fikk obeyed. He loped off to catch the others.

As Mattis started away, the drift driver softly called for his attention. "Kid," she said, and beckoned him onto the shuttle. Mattis knew he ought not to go; he was supposed to be with the others at the temple already, and besides, he didn't know the woman. She could be collecting teenagers to feed to rancors, for all he knew. But there was something trustworthy about her, something in her crossed eyes and the soft way she motioned for him to follow her that made him believe she meant to help him somehow. She closed the plug door behind him and lowered herself heavily into the driver's seat, then motioned for him to sit in the first row.

"You kids think I don't see what happens on this barge. You think I'm just the back of a head that makes the drift go!" She laughed deep in her belly.

She was right. Mattis and the others rarely paid her any attention.

"But I see everything. I seen you, Mattis Banz."

She knew his name. Did she know all the orphans? She must. But still . . . the way she said it. She put something behind his name. She gave it the kind of meaning he thought his name would have in twenty years, when people told stories about him around the galaxy.

He didn't know how to tell her all that, so he just said, "You know my name."

She laughed that deep laugh again. "You're a good kid," she said. "I see you watch out for the little 'uns, and I see you stand up for yourself. But today . . ."

Mattis looked away. Was she disappointed in him for allowing Fikk to bully him? He didn't even know the drift driver, but he didn't want to disappoint her.

"Today," she continued, "you stood up for a kid was pickin' on you. Not a good kid. Maybe a confused one, maybe one angry 'bout his circumstances. He made a fool of you, Mattis Banz." Mattis nodded. Yes, Fikk had made a fool of him. "But you didn't make him a fool in return. That shows character."

The drift driver was looking at him with—was it pride? Admiration? Whatever it was, it made Mattis feel good.

"When I see you again later, and later again, and tomorry and so on, it's best if you don't mention we had this conversation," she told him.

Mattis nodded. "But in not too long a time, we gonna have us a longer conversation."

"What about?"

"About how you can keep on showing character."

"Why not now?" he asked.

"Because now's not the time."

"Why not? I mean, it could be," Mattis said hopefully.

"Trust me," she said, and he did.

"By the way. Antha Mont."

Mattis didn't know what that was. "Antha Mont to you, as well," he insisted, figuring it must be a Skup farewell.

"Not the brightest star in the sky but means well." She grimace-smiled again and waved him off the drift shuttle with her four fingers. Then Antha Mont—her name! Of course! It came to Mattis a moment too late—closed the door on him and drifted away.

A long time later—just after the time when Mattis gave up hope that they would ever speak again, though he would linger on the drift shuttle for as long as he could after everyone had exited—Antha Mont proved true to her word. Early one morning, the shuttle arrived outside the orphan farm. It wasn't a temple day, but Mattis heard the vehicle heaving and sighing onto the landing outside. Marn was the only one awake, busy at the little stove where she prepared their morning stew.

Mattis slipped into the orphanage's doorway to see Antha Mont motion for him to come over. Running was against the rules, so he took fast little strides onto the shuttle.

"What did you do to help people this week?" she asked him.

Mattis couldn't wait to tell her. He'd carried hemmel for the little kids and even helped them harvest some. He'd gotten them dressed and made sure they were ready for temple. He didn't tell Marn when he caught Fikk and some of the other older kids shirking their duties and lounging behind the silo.

Something he said caused Antha to laugh. "We're going to have some conversations," she told him. "During temple tomorrow, you come out and see me, okay?"

"Okay," Mattis said. "I'll try."

She looked down her long nose at him. "There's

no try, Mattis Banz, hasn't been for a long time," she said. "Just do it."

"I'm not sure I can. Marn wants me to be there."

"Marn wants you to talk to me," Antha assured him. Was that true? How could he know?

Mattis shot a look back at the orphanage. Marn was in the window. She quickly dropped her head to attend to her work. Had she been watching them? Mattis thought she had.

So Mattis did as Antha said. It wasn't difficult, once he realized that Marn really did want him to talk with Antha Mont. He just waited until the congregation stood for one of the noisiest Phirmist hymns and backed up the aisle to the exit. Then he ran out of the temple and up the grassy street to where the drift was waiting for him.

Soon he was sneaking away during every trip into Lund Gourley. The conversation with Antha Mont was easy. She did most of the talking. She talked about the galaxy. She told him about the battles against the old Empire. She told him about the exploits of the Rebellion's greatest hero, Admiral Ackbar.

Sometimes Antha Mont asked him questions:

questions about himself (he tried to be a good person), about his parents (Mattis was certain they had fought in the Rebellion against the Empire, though he'd never known them), about how he'd like to make the galaxy a better place (he sure did want to).

Then, as abruptly as she had come into his life, Antha Mont was gone. The drift shuttle trundled up to them one day with a wizened Saurin as its pilot.

"What happened to Antha Mont?" Mattis asked.

"I'll ask the questions," the sour old crocodile growled back, and then, after obviously trying hard to think of a question, he finally asked, "Who is Antha Mont?" He was no help. Mattis again rode the drift in silence, did his chores, and went through his days. He didn't know what that interlude with Antha Mont had been about, but after a while he didn't think about it every day. And soon he didn't think about it every week.

Once Antha Mont and the teeming galaxy were just about gone from his thoughts, she reappeared, and she wasn't alone.

"Mattis," she said. "This is Snap Wexley. He wants to talk to you."

Snap Wexley, a likable and jocular pilot, stood

amid the seats of the drift shuttle and told Mattis all about the growing Resistance. Under the generalship of Leia Organa, the Resistance was a splinter of the New Republic military that felt the Republic wasn't taking the threat of a new dark force seriously enough. General Organa was concerned that the First Order, a group that had seceded from the Republic's senate, would someday follow in the footsteps of the Empire. She would not allow that to happen.

Mattis didn't understand all the political parts, but when Snap told Mattis "the Resistance is made up of people like you: Good people who want light in the galaxy. People who stand up to bullies. People who want to make a difference," Mattis desperately wanted to be a part of it all. And that was what it seemed like the conversation was about.

All he could think to say, however, was, "I'm only fifteen." Which wasn't even true. Mattis was fourteen.

That made Snap Wexley laugh for some reason. Mattis always seemed to be making people laugh, though he was never sure why.

"We know all about you, Banz," Wexley said. "Antha's always been good about keeping an ear to the ground for us. Now"—Mattis felt like he was standing up straighter than he ever had before as he braced for the question he hoped Wexley was about to ask him—"do you want to join the Resistance and make a difference in the galaxy?"

"Yes!" Mattis replied too loudly. He didn't have to think about it. After everything Snap Wexley had told him? After all the long philosophical conversations with Antha Mont about light and dark and power? Mattis wanted to be a hero; he always had. And the Resistance was going to show him how.

Snap Wexley laughed again and stood up. "You sure you don't have any questions for us?"

"You're sure you're the good guys?" Mattis asked.

"We definitely are," Snap said with a smile.

"Can I be a pilot like you?"

"There's no reason why you couldn't be!"

A hero *and* a pilot? His mind splashed around in the puddle of his imagination. His heart vaulted. "Then I guess my only other question is . . . how soon can we leave?"

Three weeks? Three whole weeks? It was hard enough when Antha Mont had fueled his imagination with details of a galaxy far beyond Lund Gourley and then disappeared. Knowing he was going to embark on a great adventure to *see* that galaxy, to *save* that galaxy, he had to wait three of the longest weeks of his life before Snap Wexley could return to take him to the Resistance base. It was unbearable. Worse was that he couldn't even tell anyone! The Resistance was a secret! Before Antha Mont took an interest in him, Mattis had never had a secret, not one he hadn't invented himself.

The three weeks crawled by like they were wounded badly, dragging a useless leg but soldiering on. Every meal, every day working the hemmel fields, every trip to temple (which he now had to sit through, squirming) was just a day that he was waiting to go to sleep so he could wake up again and be a day closer to leaving Lund Gourley. He took some of the smaller boys aside and encouraged them to stick up for themselves, preparing them, without saying why, for a time when he would no longer be there to protect them. He practiced flying the roto-cropper as often as he was allowed.

Mattis felt Fikk's angry eyes on him every time he got up on that roto-cropper. He could tell that

Fikk knew something had happened. Something was happening. Something was about to happen. Fikk had laid off Mattis since their confrontation, because Mattis didn't tell on him. But now Mattis was too happy for Fikk's liking and was pretending not to be. It was suspicious. The reprieve was over.

The day before Mattis was set to go, he played one last game of Rocks and Sand with Beckgam and Burm and Tchock behind the silo. Fikk was suddenly there, blocking the suns. He picked up Mattis's Emperor Stone right off the pitch, right in the middle of the game, and examined it slowly, elaborately turning it in his hard hands.

"Give that back." Beckgam stood up, surprising Fikk. Mattis was pleased. He was leaving the kids more confident than he found them. They were going to be all right. Mattis stood up, too, getting between Fikk and Beckgam. Tchock buried his face in his hands.

"Ssssomething issss happening," hissed Fikk, gesturing at Mattis as if that were an explanation. "What isss it?"

Mattis wanted to tell him. He had never wanted to tell anyone anything more than he wanted to yell in Fikk's face what the next day promised him. Mattis *needed* to tell him, but not as much as he needed not to.

"Tell me or I will take you up to the top of thissss sssilo and teach you once and for all how to fly." Fikk crushed the Emperor Stone as if it were a sand cluster.

"Leave him alone," yelled Tchock from behind his hands. Fikk snarled at him.

Mattis could imagine the conflict escalating if he didn't do something. Then he thought of just what to do.

"Fikk. Tomorrow at the center, I'll tell you everything."

"If I don't like it . . ." Fikk started.

"I'll fly away forever," Mattis finished, forcing himself not to smile.

There were two Phirmist holidays a year that were so much fun it was hard to fall asleep the night before either of them. Mattis tossed and turned in his bed that night as if both the holidays were coming in the morning. He could hear his heartbeat in his ears. He felt like his pulse would shake the bedframe. Finally, he drifted off, dreaming of flying the roto-cropper in an old battle, side by side with Luke Skywalker, under Admiral Ackbar's orders.

Mattis awoke having defeated the Empire all by himself. He barely touched his breakfast stew. He took his rucksack full of everything he owned, just as he had every day for three weeks, so as not to arouse eventual suspicion. He forced a neutral expression and *didn't* greet Antha Mont as the orphans boarded her barge. He sat next to Fikk and laughed and joked the whole way to the center, which confused the Saurin utterly.

Then, when the orphans left the drift one by one, Mattis waited for Antha Mont to tell him not to go. Instead she yelled for everyone to get off! He started to worry. He walked toward the exit as slowly as he knew how. He was nearly to the hatch. Fikk was waiting for him. Antha Mont was checking her instruments, paying no attention. Did he have something wrong? Was it because he didn't greet her? He wasn't supposed to! Had they changed their minds? Had they forgotten about him? If Antha Mont didn't say something, what was Mattis going to tell Fikk? He had one foot off the drift. Fikk licked his lips. Mattis gulped.

"Hey, Mattis Banz," Antha Mont finally said. "Sit back down. You're needed elsewhere."

"What?" asked Fikk as the door hissed closed in his grimacing face, and Antha Mont piloted them away from Lund Gourley, toward the infertile lands and whatever was next for Mattis.

They stopped at a small shack on the outskirts of Lund Gourley to pick up another passenger—a Saurin. For just a second, Mattis thought it was somehow Fikk, that they had left him at the center only to pick him up again, and he felt what little of the stew he had eaten that morning climb back up his throat.

It was not Fikk. This Saurin, Golin, had a kind, quiet demeanor. He was a little older than Mattis and didn't say anything for the whole ride. Antha Mont didn't say much, either, only told them that they were brave. Mattis wished they could be brave sooner.

They arrived in the middle of a dry field overgrown with wild grasses and brambles. There the drift landed nose to nose with the Resistance transport ship. Antha hurried Mattis and Golin off the drift and quickly said good-bye, and someone from the Resistance—it wasn't

Snap Wexley this time, but a woman of similar bearing—ushered them on board the transport, where about a dozen other kids and a couple of adults were already seated.

"Strap in, recruits," she told them as she took her own place in the cockpit. "We have a few more stops to make. Then we're headed home."

"You'd better strap in," said the Zeltron girl. Mattis had been caught in reverie, but her voice snapped him back to the present. They were on the shuttle, headed for the base. Mattis thought for a moment the girl was talking to him. She had an authoritative way of speaking that drew all attention to her. But she was addressing Klimo, who was still running around the transport.

"Why?" Klimo asked.

The Zeltron girl looked a little older than Mattis. Her red skin was a shade lighter than many Zeltrons' (Mattis had met a few as they were run through the orphan farm over the years), and her thick blue hair was pulled into a no-nonsense ponytail. She was strong, Mattis could see, but it seemed more likely that she'd knock you over with a glance. Mattis thought that was what she'd do to Klimo for daring to ask her a question, but instead she just smiled.

As she did, the entire transport ship shuddered and lunged. Klimo jounced around the passenger compartment. He squealed and chippered. The Zeltron shook her head and laughed.

They were making their descent toward the Resistance base on D'Qar. Mattis looked through the large viewport behind him. For a moment everything was gray. Then the transport lowered through the cover of clouds, and Mattis saw mountains that seemed to heave under the heavy vegetation that blanketed them. Trees threw their foliage into the sky. The planet was green and alive. It was everything the dirt farmland of Durkteel wasn't. Mattis liked it there already.

No one else seemed to stop to look at the trees. Everyone was up and moving. The pilot told them all to grab their gear and go. Mattis didn't know where. He took his rucksack and followed the others.

He didn't have much choice. The recruits were standing and moving, and if he didn't move, too, they'd trample him before trampling Klimo, who was rummaging under the seats for his belongings.

"I got it!" Klimo yelled to no one about something.

Mattis pulled the Rodian to his feet and walked him outside onto a long tarmac.

"Thanks, new best friend!" Klimo chirped, but Mattis was too spellbound to respond.

The hangar was a bigger, busier space than Mattis had ever seen. There were ships—short-range fighters and X-wing fighters and A-wing fighters—and there were people. Lots of people.

He'd never seen so many people moving toward a common goal. Pilots in orange uniforms deploying for a mission. Ground crew readying their ships. People clapping each other on the shoulders, wishing each other safe return. He saw Snap Wexley! Mattis tried to wave, but Snap was climbing into his ship. Snap knocked his knuckles on the dome of his astromech droid, smiling.

Mattis jumped aside as an orange-and-white droid came bowling through, getting in everyone's business. It paused by him, squeaked, then rolled on. Mattis watched it go, watched as that and other astromechs were loaded into their pilots' ships. Then he spotted—could it be? Yes! It was Admiral Ackbar! Mattis couldn't believe he was there! He looked around to see if anyone else was as elated to see Ackbar. The Zeltron girl shot Mattis one of those wry, condescending smiles that he could see she gave away freely. Well, what business of hers was it if Mattis was excited to be there? She should be, too! He decided he wouldn't let her, or anyone, tamp down his excitement. In fact, he'd help her liberate her own.

"I'm Mattis Banz," he said.

"Who care—" she stopped, as if she'd promised herself that she wouldn't be unnecessarily cutting. She took a deep breath, closed and opened her eyes, then said dully, "I mean, hello. I'm Lorica Demaris."

Lorica Demaris! "No way!" Mattis exclaimed.

She rolled her eyes. "I promise."

"Lorica Demaris! *You're* Lorica Demaris."

"Don't make me say it again."

"*The* Lorica Demaris!"

"I swear if you say my name again, I'm going to shove you in an astromech hole on one of these ships."

"Do you know who you are?"

"Yes, I do. Well, bye." She started out across the tarmac. Mattis figured they were probably headed the same way, so he followed. Without looking back, she said, "I don't need company."

"You blew up that cache of illegal weapons on Kergans! Amazing! We even heard about it on Durkteel! My friend Tchock thinks you're great! We all do, but he *really* does!" She didn't respond; she probably couldn't hear him over the din in the hangar. "Hey. Can you hear me? It's loud in here."

She turned back to face him. "I can hear you," she said. "So can everyone else. And you'd be doing me a real big favor, Durkteel, if you wouldn't trumpet my heroics."

"But you're a hero," Mattis said. He didn't mean for his voice to sound like a whine, but it did. "People know who you are; they should know you're who you are!"

Lorica pursed her lips and rolled her eyes again. "Please tell me you're training to be ground crew," she said.

"Nope," Mattis replied. "Pilot! What about you?"

Lorica Demaris stared at Mattis.

"What about you?" he asked louder, in case she hadn't heard him.

"Okay," she said, as if surrendering. "Thank you for your interest. It is one-sided. Please

don't follow me." Then she turned on her heel and marched away. Mattis didn't follow her. He started to feel bad for himself but was interrupted in thought when dozens of engines roared to life at once. Mattis faced the end of the tarmac, where ground crew was finishing its prep, the last of the astromechs were being deposited into fighters, and the ordnance crew was walking away.

Mattis was finally there! He was so overcome by the sight of the ships lifting off the tarmac one and two at a time, he could hardly stand. So right there on the tarmac, he dropped his rucksack and took a knee to watch the Resistance fighters rise above the forest. Someday soon, he'd be one of them.

A droid squatted next to Mattis. "Beautiful, ain't it?" he asked with an unusual lilt for a droid.

"It really is," Mattis said. The two of them shared a moment of reverie as they watched the amazing spacecraft disappear into the gray clouds.

"Ships," the droid said in awe.

"Ships," Mattis agreed. "I can't believe everyone isn't here watching this happen. It's amazing," he murmured after the last ship was out of sight.

The droid swiveled his head toward Mattis and nodded. He was unlike any droid Mattis had ever seen. He seemed to be made up of parts from about a hundred other droids and was the color of tarnished pewter, though he had some plating that was black and one navy-blue leg. His large, bug-like eyes covered most of his pointed face.

"You think *that's* something," the droid said, "you're gonna have your boots kicked off your feet just being here. You're gonna see things you never even thought about seeing."

"I'm Mattis Banz."

"Aygee-Ninety. Come on. You wanna meet my brother?"

"Sure!" Mattis stood up to follow AG-90. How could he not? He'd never met a droid's brother before.

CHAPTER

02

AG-90 WALKED QUICKLY for a droid. There was something unusual in his legs, some system of pistons Mattis had never seen before, that made AG-90 take loping strides. He might be the first droid Mattis had ever met who had a lazy confidence. And a drawl.

"Dec and me grew up on Ques. You know it? You probably don't."

Mattis didn't want to offend AG-90, but his brain was flooded with questions. How did a droid "grow up"? Was his head a J9 and his body mostly agromech? That's what he looked like. But how was that possible? Who would put those together? Who was Dec?

"Dec is your brother?" Mattis asked, since it seemed like the simplest question.

"Yep."

"I don't know Ques," Mattis said.

AG-90 laughed what sounded like an off-key song. Droids could laugh? "Ain't much to know, really," he said. "Ques is a humid swamp planet. Mostly scavengers. Some are roughnecks, y'know. Some are lum runners—you know what that is?"

Mattis shook his head. AG-90 sang that laugh again.

"Most are good folk. A community. Help each other out. Look after each other. Our folks are scrappers. Dec's a scrapper, too. Most Ques folk are. But not like Dec. Dec's a tinkerer. Can build you anything. You shoulda seen this speeder bike he tinkered up! Made them first-gen speeder bikes look like Gungan bongo subs."

Mattis wasn't sure what a Gungan bongo sub was, so he asked, "Did he build you?"

"Dec didn't have brothers or sisters and he needed lookin' out for. So Momma—she's a tinkerer, too—built Dec an older brother. That's me. What Momma didn't reckon is we look out for each other."

"You have to," Mattis said. "I mean, that's what people do."

AG-90 stopped and studied Mattis a moment. "That's what *family* does," the droid said.

Mattis shrugged. "I wouldn't know."

AG-90 cocked his head. "I ain't touching that with a Gungan's bill."

"You really don't like Gungans," Mattis observed.

"I really do not," AG-90 agreed.

They continued across the base to the small barracks at its edge. AG-90 led Mattis between the narrow buildings to a box cabin, where he threw open the door and hollered, "I found one!"

Mattis didn't know what he was one of, but he was glad to be anywhere Lorica Demaris wasn't telling him to go away.

AG-90 ushered Mattis inside and closed the door. It was a small room with a bunk bed, where a sandy-haired human boy of about Mattis's age lounged with his hands propping up his head.

"This is my brother, Dec," AG-90 said, "who I told you about."

"Hi," Mattis said.

Dec didn't get up, only smirked. Mattis would soon learn that Dec's smirk was pretty much a permanent fixture.

"This is what you brought me?" Dec said. "He doesn't look like he could guard against a baby Gungan."

"What's with you guys and Gungans?" Mattis said, almost to himself.

"You a Gungan?" Dec asked.

"Obviously not," Mattis replied.

"Then don't worry about it." Dec slid to a sitting position on the bunk and held out his hand. "Dec Hansen," he said.

"Mattis Banz."

"Find your rack and stow your sack, Banz," Dec told him, indicating he should choose a room with an empty bed and leave his bag there. "We're going on a mission."

Dec led them out behind the barracks, between a series of makeshift buildings. The entire Resistance base had a haphazard feel, like it had been cobbled together out of urgency and necessity. Like General Organa and her senior advisers knew something was happening soon, something they should prevent, so they hurried to a planet on the Outer Rim where they couldn't be found and quickly erected the base.

Mattis was worried about sneaking around, but he liked AG-90, and he wanted to like Dec, too. But what was this "mission" they were going on? Dec wasn't slowing down to explain, and he didn't stop talking long enough for Mattis to ask.

"Aygee's a good guy, and he's got a radar about who the other good people are, too," Dec said.

"I don't have an *actual* radar to detect good people," AG-90 clarified.

"I just mean Banz is probably good people. He knows there's no actual radar for that, Aygee," Dec said. Then, to Mattis, "My brother can be literal sometimes. Comes with the chrome plating. You ever meet a droid can tell a joke?"

Mattis didn't answer, but Dec didn't give him a chance to anyway.

"Aygee can tell jokes," Dec said. "But I don't know if he gets them."

"I get jokes," AG said without humor. "Don't forget I'm older. And smarter. And handsomer."

"Okay, okay. Don't get defensive."

They really did act like brothers. Dec and AG teased each other, but it was good-natured. Mattis could sense the affection between them.

"And ain't no way you're handsomer than me," Dec said over his shoulder to AG. "I'm real pretty."

"I got a better personality though," AG said. "Can't argue that. Mattis has known me twenty minutes, and he can see I got a better personality. Right, Mattis?"

Dec didn't look back at Mattis. "You better not be nodding, Banz," he said.

Mattis, who'd been nodding, stopped.

AG said, "Dec is just jealous 'cause not only do I have a better personality, but I'm a better pilot."

"You're not a pilot," Dec reminded AG.

"Not yet. But I fly. You fly, Mattis?"

Mattis said that he did, some. He didn't go into detail about how low to the ground his flying experience had been so far.

"My brother really is the best pilot I ever met," Dec said. "Some of the long-timers here don't want a droid piloting for the Resistance. They don't think droids have the instincts. Being a great pilot—like the ones you hear about in the old stories, Lando Calrissian and them? Or this guy we have now, Poe Dameron?—it's all instinct. You can't train it into 'em, and you can't program it into 'em. But Aygee's *got* instinct, because he's never had his memory wiped."

"Never?" Mattis was surprised. Wiping a droid's memory was part of basic maintenance. If you didn't wipe their memories once in a while, they developed quirks and idiosyncrasies. Which, come to think of it, was pretty much what AG was made of: quirks and idiosyncrasies.

"Never," Dec said seriously. Mattis had known Dec for only minutes, but he could tell that Dec wasn't a person who was often serious. Maybe he was only serious about his brother. "Aygee wouldn't be Aygee if you wiped him."

"Aw," AG piped up, "I'd still be a great pilot. Y'see, no matter what other parts of different kinds of droids make me up, I got the heart of an astromech. An R2 unit."

"Droids have hearts?" asked Mattis.

"Of course. I mean, kind of. Not actually. Just enough," AG explained.

"You got more heart than me, and I'm *all* heart," said Dec.

"And a better personality than you, too," AG insisted.

"Never." Dec smirked and hurried into a wide structure that was crammed with control rooms and offices. Dec was brash and confident in the way he swaggered past the periphery of the busy command center in the middle of the structure.

"Heya, Peazy!" he said, smiling and waving at a blue-plated protocol droid.

The droid raised a hand and said "My apologies, Master Dec, but I am too busy even to tell you how busy I am, and yet, I just have. Oh, dear! I have put myself farther behind. I cannot continue speaking to you. I am far too busy. Please discontinue engaging me, won't you?"

Dec shot her a salute that seemed to relieve her, and then he ducked into a corridor, past a sign that read AUTHORIZED PERSONNEL ONLY.

"This seems like the sort of place we shouldn't be," Mattis said.

Dec gave him a half smile. "What makes you say that?"

Mattis pointed to the sign.

Dec laughed and said, "Relax! I'm authorized." He said it in such a way that Mattis believed him, but only for a moment.

Down at the end of the corridor, two sentry droids as tall as Mattis stood guard.

"Aygee," Dec said. "Droid-face."

"I asked you not to call it that."

"Call *what* that?" Mattis asked.

The junk droid sighed. He pulled himself upright—AG's natural posture was a bit of a slouch—and stiffened. He took halting robotic steps into the corridor toward the two sentries.

Quickly, the sentries rolled up to him. Their rectangular eye plates glowed.

"State your business," they said in unison.

"Oh, dear!" AG replied, sounding nothing like himself at all. "I do believe you are the droids I'm looking for."

"State your business," the sentry droids repeated. One wheeled toward him, then back.

"Yes, you are just the droids. Happy day! General Organa wants to see you. I do believe she said something about a commendation!" AG sounded excited for the two sentries.

They swiveled to look at each other and rolled back and forth quickly and happily. "General Organa, you say?" asked one droid. He had a monotone, staticky voice.

"Indeed!" AG replied. When the droids again swiveled to look at each other, AG turned back to where Dec and Mattis hid in a doorway and shook his head. "Come with me."

One of the droids squealed electronically.

AG started off down a connecting corridor, away from Mattis and Dec. The two sentry droids sped after him, making positive beeping noises.

"He's good at that, huh?" Dec said, laughing. "He hates to do it."

Mattis could understand why.

Dec stopped about halfway up the corridor at a sealed door. He bent down and removed the black casing from the entry keypad, exposing buttons and wires. "I'm going in here," he said. "Your job is to watch this door."

Mattis started to protest. Dec looked up from attaching a few wires, creating a plume of electrical smoke, and shut Mattis down with a shake of his head. "I'm not doing anything wrong."

"You're breaking into this room," Mattis countered.

"Well, sure I am!" Dec said with a wink in his voice. "But it'll be great. Trust me." There was something about Dec that told Mattis he was someone to trust. That this wouldn't be much more than a silly prank.

"Besides," Dec said. "We'll never get caught if you watch this here door." He knocked on it twice, softly. "If you see anyone, don't let them come in here. Just pick Aygee up and throw him at 'em. He'll be back in a minute."

"I'm not going to throw Aygee at anyone."

"Throwing the heaviest object at the problem is lesson number one of combat," he said happily. Dec flicked a couple more wires together, and the door hissed open. He went inside, then popped his head out. "Oh, yeah, and look out for Sari."

"Who's Sari?"

"Trouble. She's got it out for me. You can't miss her. She's a bruiser. Strong as a bantha and ornery as a caged-up Kowakian monkey-lizard. Dumb, though. Strong, angry, and dumb, that's her. Ain't a good combination of things to be, Banz."

"I'll try to remember that."

"Try to remember to keep her outta here while I'm in here."

He hadn't yet ducked back inside when AG reappeared.

"You lose those trash cans?" Dec asked.

" 'Course I did," AG replied. "You tell him about Sari?"

" 'Course I did. Banz will take care of us, won't you, Banz?"

Mattis nodded. "I'll be right here."

With that, Dec popped inside and the door slid closed behind him. Mattis looked at the floor for a little bit, then leaned closer to the door. He didn't hear anything from inside the room. Mattis stole a glance up at AG, who studied Mattis coolly with his multilensed bug eyes.

"I don't know what he's up to," AG said.

That didn't make Mattis any less nervous. "Is Dec a troublemaker?"

"Oh-ho, yeah," AG said with a metallic laugh. "*Yes.*"

Mattis shifted where he stood; he eyeballed the corridor.

"But if you're his people, then you won't get in any trouble at all," AG said. "Not really."

"Am I his people?" Mattis asked.

"You're my people, so close enough."

They stood together in silence while Mattis thought about how happy that statement made him. He'd never been anyone's people before.

After another moment, though, the silence started to feel uncomfortable again. Mattis said, "You know Lorica Demaris is here?"

"I'd heard she was coming," AG said. So AG knew who she was, too. That didn't surprise

Mattis. If they'd heard about her on Durkteel, everyone had heard of Lorica Demaris.

"She was on my transport here," Mattis said, hoping to impress his new friend.

"She say anything interesting?"

Mattis thought about that. "She was kind of mean, actually."

For some reason, that made AG-90 laugh. "Aw, she's probably just nervous," he said. "Sometimes you humans get ornery when you're nervous."

"Or maybe she's just mean."

"Or maybe she's just mean," AG agreed. "Either way, I like the sound of her—Hey. Look who's comin'." AG pointed at the end of the corridor, where a hulking figure had stepped into view. Her head nearly touched the ceiling. She filled the narrow space.

"Sari?" Mattis asked. AG nodded. Mattis froze. If the girl wanted to swat past him and barge into the room where Dec was, Mattis couldn't do anything about it. She was as big as a wampa.

She didn't speak until she reached them. AG slipped behind Mattis and prodded him toward her. The girl spoke in an unnatural, low voice. "You shunnin' be here," she mumbled.

"We're . . . not?" Mattis replied.

The gargantua seemed to consider that. She tipped her dinner-plate-sized face toward the ceiling. Stringy blond hair fell away from her forehead. Then she dropped her head back down to look at them. "Nah," she said. "You're here for surely."

There was something odd about her, a studied brainlessness.

"We were going to leave," Mattis said. "But my friend here—Do you know—"

"Beebee-Ate, nice to meet you," AG said, poking his head around Mattis's shoulder. The girl scrunched up her face. She looked as if she were about to spit, laugh, or cry.

"You're not Beebee-Ate," she snarled.

"You sure?" AG asked, then made some beeps and boops.

She snorted. "You're that Dec Hansen's robot."

Then AG snorted. "No! Dec Hansen is *my* human."

"Where is he? Tell me in one piece or tell me in pieces. Up ter you."

Mattis thought quickly. Maybe he could diffuse the situation just by playing nice. "Ha-ha, come on." He chuckled, clapping her on her enormous forearm. "We're all on the same team here. Resistance, right?" She looked down at his hand, and he snatched it away.

Faster than he would have thought possible for such a giant, Sari swept her arm through the air and yanked Mattis's feet out from under him. She held him by the ankle; his head knocked against the floor, hard. The air went out of him. "You tell me where he is," she insisted.

"Hey—could you—I don't like this. Please don't—" was all he could say between breaths.

"Tell me!" the big girl grunted.

"AG? Could you—" Mattis was cut off by the girl's knocking him against the wall. He was surprised he didn't go through it.

AG said, "Oh, yeah. Hey, Sari, you don't wanna do that, do you?"

"What'm I doin'?" the girl asked dumbly.

"This!" Mattis cried. "This, this, this, please stop, please!"

AG shushed Mattis and said, "Man, keep your voice down. You'll get us in trouble." Which Mattis thought was an odd thing to say, considering they were already in trouble.

"If you don't tell me where Dec Hansen is, I'll crumple you up," Sari said.

"Please, don't," Mattis begged.

"Okay," she said. Relief flooded Mattis. "Instead, I'll throw you through that door. Last chance."

Why did bigger kids keep tossing Mattis around?

She swung him back and forth for momentum. "One," she said, swinging him away from the door, then back toward it. "The number after one." Again, back and then forth. "Three—" Even farther back that time, but when she swung him forward again, the door slid open. The hulking girl let Mattis go and he flew a few meters, right into Dec, sending them both tumbling to the ground.

"Watch it, Banz," Dec said with a sigh, pushing himself upright.

"You do what needed doing, Dec?" Sari asked. Her voice was higher and less thick. What was going on?

"Did it. Thanks, Sari." Dec was talking to her like she hadn't just caught them trespassing and who knew what else. *What was going on?*

"Sari was a real champ," AG said. "She nearly had me scared as Mattis was!" AG hadn't been scared? *Seriously, what the pfassk was going on?*

"What the pfassk is going on?" Mattis shouted.

All three huddled over him, shushing him. Dec reached out and helped Mattis to his feet.

"I'm going to lose it," Mattis said. "I mean, I've been here zero minutes, and I'm off on a secret mission, probably getting in trouble, and that's not—I'm here to do good! I don't like being tossed around! I don't know any of you, and is this"—he motioned to Sari—"*person* a guard or your friend, or what is happening here? Because I'm going to go completely moonshot if I don't—if I don't— You're smiling?"

Dec leaned against the doorway, smirking at Mattis and letting him run out of steam. "You about done?" he asked.

Mattis shrugged. He didn't trust any of them anymore, and he wouldn't give them a millimeter.

"This here's Sari Nadle. Sari's our pal."

"Hi," Sari said, smiling. Her whole demeanor had changed. Her scrunched-up face, which had seemed so angry before, was open and warm. She smoothed her blond hair across the top of her enormous head and shrugged. "I told Dec I didn't want to do brute-face, but sometimes it's the only way."

"You were great," AG insisted.

"No, I know I was great. I'm a terrific actor.

But when you're me"—she motioned to her enormous muscled body—"you always have to play the tough guy." She leaned confidentially toward Mattis and said, "I really hate violence."

"But she's a pal," Dec repeated. "And she's our people."

"How'd the new guy do?"

AG and Sari held their left hands over their right fists, right thumbs creeping out to point at Mattis.

"Really?" Dec asked, impressed.

"Didn't peep," AG told Dec.

"Not once," Sari said, and nodded approvingly at Mattis.

"Of course I didn't," Mattis said defensively. "What are you doing with your hands there?"

"It's a Quaggian gesture. Doesn't it look like a turtle head poking out of a shell?" asked Sari.

"It means 'it's great' or 'something's great.' In this instance, it means you're great," AG explained.

"He's a right guy, Dec," Sari added.

Dec took in Mattis. "Aw, he was probably too scared of you to say anything."

"He said plenty. He was really polite about it. Just nothing about you. Wouldn't budge." Sari laughed.

Mattis told all of them, "I don't tattle."

AG tried to settle Mattis down. "Dec's just being funny."

"That's not funny," Mattis said seriously to AG. He repeated it to the others. "That's not funny."

"Sure it was, Banz, or else why am I laughing?" Dec chuckled and started into the hallway.

Mattis couldn't believe Dec was just walking away, like putting Mattis through that fear and humiliation was the sort of thing he did all the time. He looked at AG, who just raised his hands as if to say, *That's my brother!*

Dec took maybe a dozen steps down the corridor by himself, then turned and came back. "Look," he said, addressing all of them. "You guys were perfect. We were having a little fun with you, Banz, and you didn't embarrass yourself or rat me out. Now I know I can trust you."

Mattis responded by making a Quaggian hand turtle.

Dec got serious. "Hey, don't use that sarcastically. What I'm saying here is that you're our kind of guy." He tapped a couple of times on AG's chest plates. "Cheer up, pals. We got away with it!"

It really did feel good having Dec call him "our

kind of guy." Relief washed over Mattis that the caper was over and they had gotten away with it.

"Mr. Hansen!" The voice came from the other end of the corridor, turning Mattis's relief into cold panic. "All of you! Stay right where you are! Miss Nadle, Aygee-Ninety, and good gracious, Mr. Banz! I say!"

Admiral Ackbar. Oh, no. He approached them with angry intensity, waving one of his big webbed hands in their direction. The two sentry droids flanked him, their eyes flashing on and off methodically. His large cranium seemed to be pulsing as he reached where they stood.

"Dec Hansen, do you think the Resistance is made up of fools?" the Mon Calamari elder statesman asked.

"I definitely don't," Dec replied. He kept his cool.

"Then don't treat us like fools!" Admiral Ackbar looked for somewhere to bang his fist but, not finding anywhere, threw his hands in the air, exasperated. "Now, you're either here to help the Resistance or you are not. This isn't a summer holiday!"

Mattis didn't say anything and checked to see what the others would do. They did nothing. Sari held her head in her enormous hands in disbelief. AG leaned against the wall and kept to himself. Only Dec dared to stare down Admiral Ackbar.

"You come with me, Mr. Hansen," Admiral Ackbar said. "The rest of you, go to your quarters. I'll deal with you all before long."

And with that he spun on his heel and marched back the way he had come. One of the sentry droids informed AG, "General Organa did not ask to see us."

The other said, "You were misinformed."

Then the sentry droids rolled behind Dec and herded him after Ackbar. Mattis, Sari, and AG-90 watched them go.

CHAPTER

03

MATTIS DIDN'T KNOW his parents, but wherever and whoever they were, he knew they were good people. He was confident that they had fought in the final battles against the evil Empire. He'd only ever shared that suspicion with one person, a three-eyed girl at the orphanage named Jinby.

"Do you have any evidence of this?" she had asked. They were both about ten years old then. Jinby was a studious sort who liked logic and reasons and math.

Mattis didn't have any evidence that his parents were great heroes of the Rebellion, but he didn't need any. He didn't care for math and had no use for reasons, and *logically*, his parents were too busy fighting the good fight against the galaxy's evil to drag their child along with them. That's *logically* why they'd left him in Marn's care. He held out only a hair-thin sliver of hope that they'd return for him someday. Instead, he figured he'd meet them when the New Republic celebrated his exploits. They'd probably surprise him at the victory parade.

"Who are these people getting on my float with me?" he'd ask, knowing full well that they were his parents but not wanting to ruin their surprise. His mother would hug him so tight it'd be hard to breathe. His father would salute him stiffly, then wobble a little and hug him even tighter.

At first, Jinby didn't agree that was probably exactly how it would go, and that was bad enough. Worse was when she conceded that, okay, probably it would happen that way. Mattis knew she didn't believe it; she was just being nice. He decided never to repeat his story.

What he had never said to anyone, ever, not even once, was that he had the Force. The Force was with Mattis.

Ever since he had been a little kid and the

Phirmists talked about the Force, he knew he had it. The Force was in everything, they said. Some people were sensitive to it. Some could wield it as a power. It was up to those people whether they used the power for good or for evil. Many didn't believe in what they thought of as an "ancient religion," but the Phirmists believed, and none more than Mattis.

Mattis had felt it swell within him. The Force. An energy that was created by and bound together all living things. Mattis would use that power to help people all over the galaxy. Just as soon as the Force manifested itself. He knew it was there, but so far, he'd been unable to push or lift objects or influence the minds of the weak (though he had tried). It was only a matter of time. He would meet someone, maybe even someone in the Resistance, who would tutor him in the ways of the Force.

But now he might never get the chance.

He sat on the hood of an unused base speeder, dangling his legs dejectedly over the pavement. A boxy yellow loader droid buzzed past. He thought he could hear it *tsk*. Mattis had really blown it.

How could he have been so stupid? He should have known better! Some hero! He'd known AG for five minutes! Why would he trust him? He'd known Dec for less. He shouldn't have trusted either of them. What Mattis should have done, on arriving at the Resistance base, was keep his head down, follow orders, and find someone who could help him realize his potential.

But no! The first thing Mattis had done was disappoint Admiral Ackbar! Admiral Ackbar had fought bravely and triumphantly against the Empire. If Mattis had inadvertently gone against Admiral Ackbar and the admiral was a good guy, what did that make Mattis? A bad guy?

The Mon Calamari statesman made his way to where Mattis sulked and stood before him. Mattis wouldn't be surprised if he was told not to bother unpacking, that he was being sent right back to Durkteel.

"You messed up," Admiral Ackbar said.

"I know." Mattis hated how weak his voice sounded.

Admiral Ackbar put a large red hand on Mattis's shoulder. "It's a bad start, Mattis," he said.

"I *know*. I'll go wait for the transport."

Admiral Ackbar stepped back. The large black pupils of his globular, jutting eyes shifted, as if

Mattis were written in a language Ackbar used to know.

"We don't want you to *leave*, Mattis," he said. "Ridiculous! Do you know the danger Snap and Antha Mont and the others courted in bringing you here? Why would we want you to leave?" Admiral Ackbar shook his head. Mattis couldn't believe that in admitting to being a disappointment, he had disappointed Ackbar even more. "It's hard to find upstanding young men and women to join the Resistance. We found you. Do you think I'm a fish-headed moron?"

"No!" Mattis said, much more confidently.

"Of course I'm not! And neither are General Organa and Commander Seastriker or anyone else in charge of this proposition. We're smart. It's why we get to be in charge. It was our decision to bring you in, and we trust our decisions." Admiral Ackbar visibly softened. "You had a bad day, Mattis. But that doesn't mean we'll give up on you."

"Thank you, sir," was all Mattis knew to say, but it didn't feel like enough.

"Come with me, son," Ackbar said, and started slowly toward a nearby building. Mattis hopped off the base speeder and joined the admiral in step. "You got caught up in that silly business before you even got your feet wet."

Admiral Ackbar walked Mattis into a small hangar where an A-wing fighter was stripped to its frame. A few maintenance droids and young ground crew banged on it with tools.

A young man maybe a few years older than Mattis approached them immediately. Unlike most of the young people Mattis had seen on the base, the man was dressed in a military fashion. The Resistance didn't really have a uniform, but he wore a martial-styled jacket, and his hair was cut close to his head. He stood up straight and nodded deferentially to Admiral Ackbar.

"Good afternoon, sir," he said.

"Jo Jerjerrod," Admiral Ackbar said. "This is your newest squad member, Mattis Banz. Mattis, Jo is your squad leader. He's among the finest the Resistance has recruited. You listen to Jo and you'll do just fine."

"Thank you, sir," Jo said. If he thought anything of Mattis, his bright blue eyes didn't betray it.

"Keep in line, Mattis," Admiral Ackbar said, waving a webbed hand and heading out.

"I'll see he does, sir," Jo said. But as soon as

Admiral Ackbar was out of sight, Jo spun on his boot heel and walked away.

"Should I—" Mattis started.

"Just stay where you are," Jo called over his shoulder. He disappeared behind the skeletal A-wing for what felt to Mattis like a long, long time. An Ugnaught in a red tunic dragged a dorsal stabilizer fin across the floor near Mattis; the fin scratched along the pavement.

"Do you—Can I help you with that?" Mattis asked. The Ugnaught snorted and glared at him.

"Don't mind Beckles," Jo said, returning. "She thinks she can do everything on her own. Maybe she can."

"Is this your fighter?" Mattis asked.

"No. I don't know whose it'll be. A Blue Squadron pilot asked me to take her apart and make sure she's *bombad*." *Bombad* was Gunganese for *great*. There was no world in the whole galaxy in which Dec and Jo would be friends, Mattis thought.

"Dec Hansen was supposed to do it," Jo continued. "He's a wild one, but he has a way with machines. Of course, he didn't stick around to help at all, despite it being a direct order from his squad leader."

"You."

"Me. The task still needs doing. So I'm doing it. Hansen will regret that."

"Okay."

"Your training starts tomorrow, Banz. Are you going to be wild like your friend?"

"Dec isn't my friend," Mattis said. "I think."

"Well, you should figure it out. You can follow orders, fall in line, and make a difference on the behalf of the Resistance, or you can be wild and we can't trust you, which means we can't use you. Give that some thought."

"I'll do the first thing," Mattis replied. "Follow orders."

"Good," Jo said. "I want to show you something."

Jo didn't wait for Mattis but turned on his heel again and exited the hangar. Mattis had to run-skip to stay a few steps behind Jo as he strode across the base. Jo didn't turn back to look at Mattis, nor did he speak any more; he walked with his back straight, and his boots clacked loudly on the tarmac.

They were in the command center when Jo finally spoke to Mattis again. "Hang back," he said. "Be quiet and watch."

The Resistance leaders were gathered around the command module. They wore stern expressions and watched as a serious-looking older man traced a pattern across a star diagram and spoke about the mission Mattis had seen begin that morning. Mattis picked out a label, Nardin, though whether it was a person or place, he could not discern. Then Mattis heard a name he knew well from the old stories: Luke Skywalker. Was Luke Skywalker part of the Resistance? Could Luke Skywalker train Mattis to be a hero, too?

Mattis had a lot of questions, but he was an old pro at what they at the orphan farm called the Competitive Silence Challenge. He could go for up to five minutes without speaking. Six if it meant impressing his squad leader.

The Resistance leaders seemed frustrated. They'd gotten word from their mission commander that the team hadn't met its objective. The mission would take more time, which meant a greater likelihood that the Resistance would be discovered by its enemies. Plans were made and contingencies were considered. Mattis had many questions, and he was sure he had been quiet for an hour. Not even the Competitive Silence Challenge *champion* could do that.

As if Jo could tell Mattis was at the limit of his ability to stay quiet, he took Mattis out into the hangar and sat him down on a makeshift bench surrounded by a collection of greasy tools. An X-wing fighter had taken off from that spot just hours before. There was no one else around.

"Do you know what the First Order is?" Jo asked him. Mattis remembered hearing about the First Order from Snap, but Jo did not wait for a reply. "The First Order started out as a splinter group of the Empire. After the Battle of Jakku, they broke off and gained a modicum of respectability. They were even part of the New Republic for a while. But they've been planning something. An awakening of power and destruction. That's what General Organa says, and she's seen it before. General Organa helped Admiral Ackbar defeat the Empire a generation ago."

Mattis tried not to roll his eyes. Of course he knew who General Organa was.

"We need to stop the First Order, Mattis. Us. We're not playing a game here. The First Order is bad. They are *bad people*. It's going to take discipline and training to stop them before they do some real damage. Discipline and training. You think your friend Dec has discipline?"

Mattis could feel Jo's hatred for their enemy under his own skin. It felt hot and anxious. Dec wasn't the kind of person who could defeat them. Dec broke rules.

"I can't hear you," Jo said. "Do you think Dec Hansen has discipline?"

"No!" Mattis said, louder than he'd said anything since arriving on the base.

"That's it. Good. I will teach you to follow orders. I will teach you discipline and, in return, you will help me help Admiral Ackbar and General Organa protect the galaxy. Do you understand me?"

Mattis nodded, excited. He wanted to salute, but he didn't want to salute wrong.

"Do you understand me, Mattis?"

"Yes!" Mattis shouted, saluting.

Jo smiled at Mattis's salute. Mattis couldn't tell if it was because he'd done it perfectly or wrong. Rather than ask, he decided he'd done it perfectly. Jo stalked past Mattis and told him to fall in, which meant follow him.

Lorica Demaris was waiting for them in an area called the Yard, despite its bearing no more resemblance to a yard than a wampa did to a pot of beans. The Yard was a small converted hangar in a remote corner of the base. A series of soggy knolls rolled off its back wall like ocean waves. Mattis could hear the hoots and shrills of local birds and longed to identify them from the books he'd read, but the Yard was windowless. It was spare save for two short rows of benches, various types of flight and combat equipment, and against one wall, a locked store of weapons.

Jo marched Mattis into the Yard, which was dim with artificial light. Maybe to sharpen their combat senses? Or maybe the Resistance didn't have the power to generate electricity in every corner of its base. When Jo introduced Lorica to Mattis, she just raised an eyebrow and said, "Oh, we've met. How's it going, Durkteel?"

Jo told him, "The Resistance is pleased to have Lorica on board. We know her reputation, of course."

"Oh, does she have a reputation?" Mattis asked, matching Lorica's disinterest.

Jo told Mattis that she did indeed and went into details, once again telling Mattis things he already knew. Jo seemed immune to sarcasm.

"He knows, Jo," Lorica said, cutting him off. "He told me who I was a few times when we got here."

"I was just surprised. I figured you'd have joined the Resistance ages ago," Mattis said to Lorica. "I mean, you being you."

"Being *me*?" She said it as if it were an insult.

"Lorica was brought in the same way you were, most likely," Jo said. "Though probably the recruiters had to work a little harder to dig you up, Mattis."

"My reputation preceded me, I guess," Lorica said. "Jo was sent down to talk to me." She lowered her eyes when she mentioned Jo. It made Mattis feel intrusive and jealous, for some reason.

"Lorica was a natural fit for the Resistance. I could tell in just the few times we spoke that she'd be a good soldier."

"Already done some damage to some bad guys," Mattis said, nodding.

"She has discipline," Jo corrected him. "The things we talked about. It'll take more than well-placed bombs to take down the First Order. You'd do well to follow Lorica's lead. I'll see you both at sunrise." With that, Jo about-faced and stalked out of the Yard.

"He's got a lot to prove." Lorica shook her head.

"Is that true? Why?"

She glared at him. "I don't know," she said. "I just know how people are."

Mattis stuck up his hands innocently. "Okay," he said. "You know him better than I do."

"I don't know anyone."

Mattis didn't know what to say in response, so he took in the Yard. He might as well get used to it. He'd be there for the foreseeable future. He looked for the birds but didn't spot any of them. He realized his focus had drifted when Lorica broke the silence. "Did you really break into General Leia's rooms?"

Mattis stumbled back a few steps. "Those were General *Leia's* rooms?" he said. Dec had been more reckless than Mattis had known. The general's quarters! It was a wonder Admiral Ackbar hadn't court-martialed them! If court-martialing was something they even did there. Maybe he was lucky they didn't.

Lorica was still staring at him. "I d-didn't," he stammered. "I mean, yes—not me—Dec did. I just kept watch—I mean—I just got here. You saw me get here! You just got here. I mean—"

"You're going to be so much trouble, aren't you?" There was menace but also a smile in her voice.

"Not if I can help it." He sighed. "Can I ask you a real honest question?"

Lorica consented.

"Do you know if the Resistance has bathrooms? I haven't seen any, and I've never needed one more."

That made Lorica laugh. "Follow me," she said. They left the Yard. Lorica led him to a row of doors, each with a symbol of a drop of water on it. "Any more questions?"

"Did you always know you were going to be a hero?"

"Don't push it," she told him, and then pointed. "Barracks are that way, mess hall's over there. Past that, you're on your own. See you at sunrise, Durkteel."

Mattis was exhausted. He made his way back to his bunk directly. His rucksack was where he'd left it, and he saw that someone had claimed the bottom bed.

"Best friend?" Klimo, the enthusiastic Rodian, chirruped. He leaped up and smacked Mattis hard on the back. "I knew that was your bag! I found it! It took some looking, but I found it! We're bunkmates, best friend! This will be so exciting! So much adventure for us!"

Klimo pushed Mattis down on the empty bunk and laughed loudly. "Tell me all about your life! We will stay up all night as best friends do! Is it true that you broke into the general's rooms?"

CHAPTER

04

MATTIS AWOKE IN the dark, thrumming. It was nearly dawn and he was ready for a real first day. After the day before, he felt he had something to prove, and he was ready to prove it. He knew he could make a difference to the Resistance. If he had to follow Jo's orders to the letter, then that's what he'd do, and he'd make Lorica like him while he did it.

Mattis slid out of his bunk quietly, eager to head down to the Yard. No sooner had he put his feet to the floor, though, than the light snapped on and Klimo rolled out of his bunk in a pile of limbs and noise.

"Today is our first day!" he shouted.

Mattis nodded. "Yep, that's right," he said, demonstrating acceptable volume.

"Should we go to the Yard? Should we be early to first-day training, Mattis? Do you want to race there?"

Mattis lit up with an idea. "Sure," he said. "I'll race you." He slipped into his boots, then said, "Ready-set-go."

Klimo bounded from the bunk, a nasal shriek like a disappearing siren following him out into the base. Mattis laughed to himself and followed, walking. Klimo would win the race. And Mattis would have a few moments to himself before training began.

When Mattis arrived at the Yard, Klimo was waiting for him, hands on his knobby knees, panting. "Hoo-boy, best friend! You gave me a run for my credits!"

Lorica Demaris was already there, and laughed at Klimo's jovial chumminess with Mattis. Some of the other squad members laughed, too.

The Yard wasn't bare as it had been the night before. Someone, probably Jo, had woken early to set up what looked like an elaborate obstacle course. The room was divided into corridors via sturdy-looking barricades. Every few meters, a large metal door was affixed between them. Two sentry droids methodically monitored the makeshift corridors.

The squad that fell under Jo's command was a varied crew. Besides Lorica and Klimo, there was a pair of round-headed, tusked Aqualish boys. One was tall and gangly, and the other was short and pudgy. There was a human girl who wore an insignia from the planet Ganthel. Mattis would have to be wary of her; Core planet natives were usually aristocratic snobs. Mattis suspected Jo was also from the Core, what with his superior attitude and fanatical rule-following. A brown-and-white-furred, stick-thin alien girl with a dog snout hung around Lorica, who paid her little mind. Another kid Mattis took for a human around his age removed his cap, and Mattis saw two blunt horns sticking out of his shaggy black hair.

Mattis had been right: everyone had heard of Lorica. Everyone on the squad was looking at her, though nobody was making eye contact. Her name bubbled to the surface of every quiet conversation. She pointedly ignored it.

Jo cleared his throat and addressed them all.

"My name is Jo Jerjerrod. I am your squad leader. My contempt for the First Order is absolute. You want to be fighter pilots. Some of you will be. It's important, for the next days and weeks and months, that you learn your part in the Resistance. Every one of you, everyone on this base has a role to fulfill. With my help you will fulfill yours to the fullest."

A positive energy overtook the group, and they all drew a bit closer to one another.

"Where's Hansen?" Jo asked, looking directly at Mattis.

"I don't know. Why would *I* know?"

"You were the last to have eyes on me, Banz. That's why!" Dec hailed him as he, AG, and Sari walked in. "Jerjerrod, I know you're a stickler for time, but this session isn't supposed to start until the crack of dawn and dawn hasn't cracked yet. How long till the dawn cracks, Aygee?"

"Couple seconds after I finish saying . . . *this*."

"So about now, then?" Dec asked, smirking as if it were his job.

AG made a sound like he was sucking teeth he didn't have with air he didn't breathe. "No, you missed it."

"We're on time," Sari said, winking at Mattis.

Dec approached with the other two flanking him, like a formation of X-wing fighters attacking an enemy base. "Everyone ready to get started?" he asked. He grinned openly at Mattis. Mattis looked away.

"Fall in with the squad," Jo said sharply.

Dec bobbed his head coolly and stood by the Aqualish boys, who grunted. Mattis didn't know what the grunts meant—*nice to meet you* or *go away*—but Dec didn't seem to mind them either way. He laughed like they'd told a joke. Then, noticing Lorica, Dec exclaimed, "Hey, you're Lorica Demaris!"

Lorica winced. Sari looked impressed. AG didn't. "I thought you'd be redder," the droid said.

Jo ran his eleven charges through training exercises. Mattis had heard stories of how the Empire used to punish and torture people. None of that sounded so bad compared with the Resistance training. Every part of Mattis burned, tingled, and wanted to fall off. He had never sweated with such purpose. To his credit, Jo joined in on every exercise of the seeming thousands he asked of his squad. Every second set was push-ups. AG did the exercises, as well, for solidarity. The only good thing Mattis could say about the training was that he was pleased to get it all out of the way on the first day. It felt like they had done enough to last each of them an entire lifetime. After the pudgy Aquilish boy fainted, Jo finished the session for the day, promising that it would come to be everyone's favorite morning ritual in the months that followed. Mattis hated that idea so much.

Mattis cheered right up, though, when Jo told them the next part of training was a war game. "Each of you will be given an assignment designed to accentuate your strengths and your role in this squad. Your goal is this map." Jo held up a small piece of scrap metal.

"That's not a map," Klimo said.

"Pretend it's a map," Jo ordered.

"Aye-aye!" Klimo saluted.

Mattis didn't take his eyes from Jo. He wanted to be a good soldier. He wondered what role Jo would find for him in the training exercise.

Jo dictated positions to some of the others—transport, code breaking on the security-locked doors—and he told Lorica she'd be mission leader. She nodded confidently. Jo told Mattis, "You're the lookout. Hang back, make sure the sentry droids don't catch you all in action. Think you can handle that?"

That made Dec laugh. "Banz can handle that all right, chief."

Jo glared at Dec. "You'll be Mattis's cohort. Stay two steps behind him. Aygee-Ninety, your job is to disarm those sentry droids should they discover any of you."

AG drawled, "Aye-aye."

"Finally," Jo said, "some of those security locks aren't going to be cracked. Which is where you come in, Sari. You're the muscle. Knock those doors in."

Sari's eyes narrowed. "I can slice the codes on those doors."

Jo shook his head. "You're the muscle, Sari. Look at you."

Dec piped up, "Chief, Sari's a genius. She can slice her way into anything."

"I'll second that," AG said. "Ain't the point to be clandestine?"

"That's not the exercise," Jo said tightly.

"You want muscle? Flex for him, Aygee." Dec prodded his brother, who put his metal arm up in imitation of a flexing motion.

"You tell a door I'm coming," AG said, "it

starts shaking on its hinges. Let me at a door."

Mattis felt his neck get hot. "Jo's the squad leader," he mumbled. He didn't mean to mumble it. He meant to say it with confidence. Dec heard him anyway.

"You heard Banz; Jo's the leader," Dec chided at the volume Mattis intended.

"Are you really causing discord in my squad?" Jo asked Dec. "So soon after getting on Admiral Ackbar's bad side and derelicting your duty to that A-wing yesterday?"

"You prefer I wait a few days? So you can see who's wrapped around your finger, playing their so-called role and takin' away the stuff that made the Resistance want us on board in the first place?" Dec's swamp accent came on strong when he was agitated.

"It's okay, Dec," Sari said, looking at the floor. "I'm the muscle. It's fine."

"It *ain't* fine."

Sari put a big hand on Dec's shoulder. "It's *fine.*"

Dec bobbed his head a couple of times, rebuilding his wall of laid-back confidence. "Just fine," he said. "Any further orders, *sir*, or can we get on with it?"

If Jo was pleased that he'd won the confrontation, he didn't betray it. He just barked at them to take positions and begin the exercise. So they did, and Mattis didn't let the sentry droids see them, and Sari knocked down doors, and Lorica called out commands, and Dec dragged himself along behind Mattis, not talking much to anyone. But he was thinking. Mattis could see the turbines rotating.

The weeks passed in that way. J-Squadron, as they were soon called, followed Jo's orders. He put them through their paces with those horrible exercises and other ones that got them to stretch mentally and practice limited spy craft or combat. They didn't, however, get to fly.

It was a sore point among most of them.

"He'll let us take a fighter out when we're ready," Lorica said whenever they would complain.

None of them wanted to get into a cockpit as badly as AG did. "I was ready before we got here," he'd counter. Their arguments would end in a stalemate, because, really, it was up to Jo. If he didn't want them flying, then they were grounded.

They were, however, ordered to use the flight simulator. They'd each climb into what looked

like half a giant shell. It was soft and a little viscous inside and out. The top looked like an open,
four-petaled flower. The "pilot" sat in the middle. It was a little tight for everyone but Klimo. A
small screen projected from a control panel; that
was a simulation of their cockpit module.

"It ain't flyin'" was all AG would say about it.

Mattis liked the simulation. He felt himself
becoming a better, more confident pilot. He listened to Jo and Lorica as they shouted commands
and did his best to react swiftly. He liked sim-
flying in formation with J-Squadron. He liked
when they all bore down on a target and destroyed
it together as a team. He felt a fellowship with
them then, even if the squad still felt tenuous in
the nonsimulated world.

It was maybe their fifth time in the flight
simulator when Dec ruined that feeling. They
were running a scenario in which the flanking attackers would defend the lead ship as war
droids fired at them from the ground of a desert
planet. Green Leader, which was Lorica, would
fire on the war droids. It was a tight-formation
attack, a scenario J-Squadron had struggled with
in previous sims. They tended to fly either too far

apart, thus rendering themselves unable to properly defend Green Leader, or too close together, knocking one or another of them off course.

This time, they were flying right. Lorica was telling them when to lay down suppressing fire so she could swoop in low and sweep the war droids. On the fourth pass, Dec broke formation and sped ahead of the rest of them. As he deployed his proton torpedoes while simultaneously gunning the war droids with his blaster cannon, he threw up so much smoke and sand that they lost him on their tracking computers. One of the Aqualish boys—the gangly one, whose name was Haal—tottered his fighter and clipped Mattis's wing; it was all Mattis could do to regain control and stay in the sloppy formation in which they found themselves as they emerged from Dec's chaos cloud.

Mattis hadn't realized that both Jo and Lorica were shouting at Dec, as all he'd heard were the sounds of simulated explosions and squawking war droids.

"What in the forest moon of Endor was that?" Jo had his finger in Dec's face. Dec wore a huge smile.

"Yee-haw," said Dec. "We finished off those war droids, and we're all safe as a landing. Mission achieved, chief."

"Mission *not* achieved!" Jo was never so focused as when he was furious. "The mission was to execute Lorica's commands! Your squadron could be dead right now because of you, Hansen!"

Dec looked around at J-Squadron. "Is everyone fine?" Only AG responded with a yep. "Everyone's fine," Dec insisted.

"You couldn't know they would be!" Lorica threw her helmet aside and charged Dec, shoving him in the chest. He fell back into his pod.

"What was that for?"

"Stand down, Lorica," Jo said.

She was fuming. Her skin turned a deeper red. "You didn't follow orders. Haal was knocking around formation because you threw up smoke and sand and whatever else. You do that in the field, and we're dead."

"We're not dead!" Dec said defensively. "I had Aygee on my tail, and we've run this kind of scenario for real hundreds of times down in the swamp."

AG tilted his head. "Well, to be honest, it was

on speeder bikes and we were taking shots at slime crabs for dinner, but it worked out the same."

"You don't even eat dinner," Jo seethed.

"You don't know what meals I don't eat!" AG shot back.

Jo turned his attention back to Dec. "You never fly out of formation. Ever."

"Yeah, I do, chief! I do all the time. Always have. Especially when formation is slowin' me down."

"That's *nutsen*," Jo said, leaning into the Gungan word for *crazy*.

"You can try eggin' me on like that, but you're the angry fella here, not me." Dec all but tweaked his nose. "I'm cool as a dead star, and all you got to show for it is you're wrong and you sound dumb as a Gungan."

Jo got even madder. "My best *friend* is a Gungan, and he's worth a hundred of you and two hundred of your 'brother.'" Jo's Gungan button didn't work on Dec, but in that moment, he saw one that might. "*Your brother*, who I shouldn't even let in the sim, because droids *aren't* pilots."

"Aygee is a pilot," Dec said quietly, some of his confident swagger gone. That button worked.

"Don't worry about it," AG said to Dec.

"I said to you, *chief*, that my brother is a pilot." Dec stood nose to nose with the squad leader.

"He's a robot." Jo was cool now. "He might make a serviceable astromech if his memory were wiped."

Dec glared, and AG reached out to put a hand on him. Dec shook him off.

"Then he could be programmed for flight and discipline," Jo continued. "Too bad we can't reprogram you, too."

"No one. Is gettin'. Reprogrammed," Dec said. His hands balled into fists, and Mattis was afraid he would take a swing at Jo.

"Is he going to hit him?" asked Klimo.

Lorica pushed Dec and Jo apart. "Insubordination. Fifty push-ups, Dec," she said sharply.

Dec just kept glowering at Jo, who liked the sound of push-ups. "All right. If Dec won't do his own push-ups," he said, "everyone else will. Fifty push-ups, everyone."

Dec looked at Sari, grimacing as she got into push-up position. He looked at AG, then at Mattis, his people, and he dropped to the ground. "Don't bother, everyone. I do my own push-ups. You want fifty? I can give you a hundred."

Jo shook his head. "Everyone give me a hundred, except Dec. Dec, you go ahead and do whatever you want. That's what you're best at."

Dec ignored that and started his hundred push-ups.

"Keep at it," Jo said, looking down at them all. "I'll see you in the morning." For once, Jo did not do the exercise with everyone else.

Once Jo had gone, a couple of J-Squadron members tapered off their push-ups, but Lorica reminded them that, while it was Dec's fault, they did all have to follow orders. "Why can't you just do the same?" she asked Dec between puffs.

"Because," Dec said, panting hard himself. "That's no way to win a war."

"Jo is—*hff*—training us to win a war," she said.

"No," Dec said. "Jo doesn't see us, not really. AG is the best pilot we got, and Jo's not letting him be Green Leader. No offense."

"All kinds of offense taken," Lorica said.

"He's making Sari knock down walls. That ain't what Sari does. And Banz is a go-getter. . . . Lookit him. All you need to do is point him. Who would waste Banz's time by making him keep watch?"

"You did," Lorica reminded him.

"Yeah, but that was before I knew him. That was foolin' around. My point is, Jo takes away what's—*hff*—unique about each of us, we're for sure gonna lose any battle we're in." He doubled the pace of his push-ups, then abruptly hopped to his feet. "That's two hundred," he said. He was breathing heavily and wiping the sweat from his face. "What're you at?"

Lorica hopped up, too. "Two hundred," she said dryly.

"Fine," he said, and sauntered out. AG followed. Lorica watched the rest of them, then she left, too. Five more members of J-Squadron finished in turn, leaving Klimo, Mattis, and Sari—the worst at push-ups—to complete their punishment. Klimo screamed and collapsed. In seconds, he was lightly snoring, completely exhausted by the workout.

Mattis finished his set and rolled onto his side. "I'm done," he said. "I hate both of them."

Sari sat down beside Mattis. "Don't hate Dec," she said. "Dec likes you a lot."

"He could've gotten us all killed. That's not why I came here. I prefer being alive. He doesn't care about anyone."

Sari's big eyes got bigger. She bit her lip, considering whether or not to say something.

"What?" Mattis asked.

"Dec needs friends who'll watch his back. He doesn't take to people easily. He likes me, but—" She laughed quietly. "Everybody likes me, once they're not afraid of me."

"Why would I watch his back?"

She sighed deeply. It had the sound of a low motor dying down. "You know why Dec broke into General Organa's rooms that first day you were here?"

Mattis shrugged. "To make some trouble."

"No," Sari said. "It was to get Aygee assigned to a bunk."

"Aygee didn't have a bunk?"

"He didn't. The Resistance didn't give him one. They think he's just a droid. And anyway, they've got their hands full with more important stuff than figuring out where the recruits are supposed to lay their heads."

"But Aygee doesn't sleep, right? He's not 'just a droid,' but he's still a droid."

Sari smiled. "He doesn't sleep, of course not. He powers down, and the brothers both prefer he do it in a bunk rather than standing in a corner like the other droids. He's got stuff. Belongings. Mementos from his home planet. Things that remind him of his childhood with Dec. He's still a droid, yes, but he's not *just* a droid. Do you see?"

Sari rose and headed for the door.

Mattis stayed on the ground and watched her head out. "Sari," he said.

She turned and waited. He didn't know what to say. He was moved by what she had told him, how she had told him, that she had trusted him. "See you at mess, huh?" he said, finally. She nodded, then turned back around and left.

Mattis stayed on the floor a little longer, catching his breath. He woke Klimo, and they went to get ready for dinner.

Later, Mattis made his way across the mess hall, holding his tray loaded with rations. Klimo followed him. Jo sat with some of the other squad leaders, Lorica, and the Aqualish boys. At a smaller table in a remote corner, Dec, Sari, AG, and J'mi, the slight alien girl with the mottled fur and protruding snout, laughed and ate their rations. Mattis usually sat at the end of Jo's table. There he could show his allegiance to Jo and the Resistance command but keep well removed from actual conversation. That night, though, he crossed the mess and sat down with Dec and the others.

"You mind?" he asked before sitting.

"'Course not. You and your Rodian are always welcome," Dec said, opening his arms. "Grab a bench. J'mi is just telling us about life back on Regor-Mada."

As he sat, Mattis said quietly, "Sari told me what you did for Aygee. That's . . . good of you."

Dec waved away Mattis's praise. "We take care of each other," Dec said, then turned back to J'mi and the others. "Tell us about that river you fell in. It makes you sound like a dope, and that makes me laugh."

CHAPTER
05

A MONTH PASSED. Mattis, Dec, AG, and Sari fell into an easy friendship, only occasionally put aside for push-ups, during which nobody liked anybody and everybody hated everything. Their friendship was only sometimes strained because of Mattis's desire to follow Jo's orders, and Jo had a lot of orders. Jo saw that Mattis was growing close with Dec and the others and rode Mattis harder for it. Mattis took every order, though. As much as he wanted to be friends with his gang, he wanted to do as Jo told him so that one day he would be the hero he dreamed of being.

———

There was tension all across the base. The mission on which the fighter pilots had left when Mattis arrived was still active. It was taking longer than anyone had anticipated. Mattis often saw Admiral Ackbar pacing around, worriedly muttering to himself. From what Mattis could piece together from overheard whispers between Jo, Lorica, and the Ganthelian girl in J-Squadron—her name was Leeson Juben—the mission leader had sent word that the fighters could return unannounced. This was unusual for a well-orchestrated undertaking. But it meant that they were still out looking for whatever it was they were looking for. The absence of so many Resistance pilots and fighters was making everyone snippy and sloppy. What conversation didn't happen behind closed doors was terse and short-tempered.

Klimo, too, was becoming a problem. His enthusiasm for their "adventure" and "best-friendship" hadn't waned since they arrived. Mattis couldn't shake him. From the time Mattis woke up in the morning to the time he returned to his bunk at night, Klimo was at his heels, always underfoot despite being one step behind. He was Mattis's green shadow. The others teased him about his "best friend."

One night, Dec knocked gently on the door of Mattis's room before sliding it open. On the first knock, Klimo leaped from his bunk into a squat on the floor, his hands out in front of him as if he were holding a blaster on Dec, who was already inside.

"*P'kow p'kow!*" Klimo imitated a blaster.

"If I was coming to blast you, I'd have blasted you before you even landed," Dec said to Klimo, grinning.

Klimo shook his head. "No way, friend's friend! Klimo is fast."

"If you're fast at all, it's in a one-step-behind sort of way," Dec said.

Mattis was still rubbing sleep from his eyes as Dec crossed the small room and snapped on the light.

"Wakey-wakey, Banz," Dec said. "We're gonna have some fun tonight."

Mattis dropped his head back onto his pillow. "No, please."

AG and Sari crowded into the narrow barracks and hung near the doorway.

"It's nothing bad," Sari said.

Mattis covered his face with his hand. Farming back on Durkteel hadn't kept him awake as much as life on the base. "If it weren't bad," he said, "we wouldn't have to do it in the middle of the night."

"Dec is hungry," AG reported.

Mattis rolled onto his side and raised his eyebrows at Dec. "And you can't wait until morning?"

"I'll starve to death if I wait till morning. You want that on your conscience?" It was no use arguing. Dec was dug in. What was the worst that could happen? They wouldn't be kicked out for sneaking over to the mess hall and swiping a few ears of Lemus corn.

"What's the 'mission'?" Mattis asked.

Dec laughed again. "Easy as pie," he said. "Hubbard pie, specifically." Earlier that week, their dinner rations had included a pie about the size of Mattis's palm. Every single man, woman, and alien in the Resistance mess that night had emitted a squeal of glee heard halfway across the galaxy.

"I'm in," Mattis said.

That made everyone laugh. They'd watched for probably an hour as Mattis savored his Hubbard pie. He'd never had anything so warm and sweet.

"They gotta have more, right?" Dec said. "It's

nothing for Sari to slice into the mess. We'll just take one apiece. Or two."

"One," Mattis said. He didn't want them getting carried away.

"You comin', greenie?" Dec asked Klimo.

Klimo jumped up and down. Of course he was going. "Let's sneak into the mess hall!" he yelled. Mattis warned him that he'd have to keep quiet, and a moment later, they were sneaking to the mess hall. A moment after that, Klimo followed them. One step behind.

The base at night was dark and silent. A month before, there would have been activity at all hours. But with all the training and fretting over missions, when the Resistance slept, it slept hard. There were a few hours each night that all Mattis could hear was the whir and hum of sentry droids. Even the protocol droids powered down for the night.

They crept noiselessly, bunched in a group behind Dec. The only sound they heard was the light clanking of AG's body. It sounded thunderous to Mattis, and he was sure that Admiral Ackbar would burst from his quarters and reprimand them all at any moment.

But he didn't. What stopped them was Dec, ducking behind some transport ships. The others followed suit, unsure exactly why. It took Mattis a moment to realize that Dec was pointing to one of the main command structures. His eyes adjusted to the dim light on the building just in time to see someone scan a security card and slip inside.

"Who was that?" Mattis whispered.

"That was Jo," Dec said.

"No way," Mattis said.

Dec turned to the group. "One of you must've seen. That was Jo."

They all looked at each other. Finally, AG nodded. "It was," he said. "I saw him, too." But whether it was because he saw Jo or because he would always back up his brother, nobody could discern.

It was proof enough for Klimo, who waved and started to say something, probably "Hello, Jo." Quick as lightspeed, Dec's hand shot up and gripped Klimo's snout tight.

Dec held a finger to his own lips and asked with his eyes if Klimo understood to be silent. The Rodian nodded as best he could, and Dec slowly unwrapped his fingers from Klimo's weird mouth situation.

"Why would Jo sneak around?" Sari asked.

"He sure ain't out for Hubbard pies," Dec said. "Mess is all the way down there. That's a communications center in there. Intragalactic. Highly restricted."

"Jo doesn't have clearance." Sari looked worried.

"We gotta go in after him," Dec said.

"Why?" asked Mattis. "There's no way Jo, if it even was Jo, is up to anything he isn't supposed to be."

Dec and AG shared a look that said, *Poor Mattis*.

"What? What am I missing?"

"Always suspect the person you least suspect."

"Of what? And why?"

There was every chance Dec was making it all up as he was going along, but he gave no indication. He said, "Of everything. There's always a reason they're trying to throw you off their scent. Number two lesson after 'If you're in trouble, throw the nearest large object at the problem' is never, *ever* completely trust someone you can completely trust."

"Wait, does that mean that because you can trust me . . . you can't trust me?"

Dec and AG shared that *poor Mattis* look again.

"I can get us in," Sari said, and started off for the communications center door, staring down the swipe-pad door lock and cracking her considerable knuckles. The others followed.

"I have a good feeling about this!" Klimo nervously whisper-yelled in Mattis's ear.

Mattis shushed Klimo, and then Dec and AG shushed Mattis. Sari shushed them all.

She entered a code that slid the door lock's exterior to the side and into the programming interface.

"Are you bypassing the—" AG-90 started to ask.

"Rerouting it."

"Wow! You think you can crack the—"

"I know I can."

"You could enter a—" AG started again.

"Yeah." Sari cut him off. "If I had all night and a Murr rabbit's foot."

"Sure," AG conceded, "but have you thought of a digital scrape that jump-jacks the main connect?"

Sari's eyes narrowed. "Maybe that would have worked, too," she said coolly as the door unlocked. "Didn't need it, though."

The door slid open to reveal a long corridor

lined with rooms, all dark except the last one, which emitted a faint light. Whether it was Jo or not, *someone* was in there, off hours, using the intragalactic communications center.

"Sneak-race you, bro!" AG whisper-yelled as he quickly tiptoed in.

Dec frowned and said as loud as he could whisper, "AG, get back here. Sari, get that door shut again. And, greenie? No matter what you do, don't yell—"

"Lorica!" Klimo cried. Fortunately, his shout covered the sound of the door sliding closed—with AG still on the other side of it. Lorica, wearing military pajamas, was heading their way.

"Lorica," Sari said quietly as the other girl approached them. "What are you even doing out here?"

"Are you sleepwalking?" Mattis asked, thinking quickly. "Sometimes Klimo sleepwalks. We were just—getting him. Out of . . . sleepwalking."

Klimo squeezed his round black eyes shut and stretched his arms out in front of him. "I was sleepwalking!" he said too loudly.

"Can you whisper?" Mattis asked.

"I am whispering!" Klimo cried.

"Did you guys see Jo?" Lorica asked. She showed no interest in either their lies or reasons for being out in the middle of the night.

"Jo Jerjerrod?" Mattis played dumb. Lorica fixed him with a caustic stare. "Ha-ha! Yes. I mean, yes, of course that's who you mean. But no. We haven't seen him." An impatient silence hung over the group. "Dec?"

"Lor."

"Don't call me that."

"*Mizz* Demaris, pardon *me*," Dec continued. "What's your boyfriend, Jo, gonna do when he finds you out wandering the base at this hour?"

"He's not my boyfriend," Lorica told him, and turned to the security doors. She looked at the swipe pad. She didn't have a security card any more than the rest of them did.

Mattis couldn't help feeling a softness and sensitivity whenever Lorica was around, despite her obvious dislike of him. That was the only way he could explain what he said next. "It's hard here."

The others all looked at him as if he'd dropped a dead dianoga in the middle of the conversation.

"What did you say?" Lorica asked.

"Banz, take a break," Dec said pleasantly.

But Mattis didn't want a break. Calmness had overcome him when Lorica arrived, which was not how he ought to have felt. As was so often the case when he was in her presence, he felt his heart open up and his eyes get watery. Not from upset or ire but just from . . . he didn't know what. Was it the Force, Mattis wondered? Was Lorica Force-sensitive, and was she opening his mind and heart to its ways? He trusted that was the case. So he repeated himself: "It's hard here."

Another odd silence.

Until Lorica said, "It is. It's . . . it's really difficult."

The others didn't look at her, too afraid to break whatever spell was currently over them. But Mattis did. "Sometimes I don't think I can handle it," he told her. "Honestly. You and Jo—you guys are so tough, so disciplined. You're meant for this. Sometimes I don't think I know anything but cutting hemmel. And that's no help against the First Order."

"I don't always feel meant for it," Lorica said. When she spoke, it seemed to Mattis as if she and he were the only people on the base. Maybe on the whole planet.

But then Dec spoke up, too. His voice was

gentler than Mattis had ever heard it before. "Me too," he said. "I want to do this right, y'know? I want to be as much help to the fight as I can be, but—but the ways don't always make sense."

Sari nodded and mumbled an agreement. "I have things to offer," she said. "But I don't know what's the right way."

Klimo slapped Mattis on the back and said, "I am glad they are all my friends. It helps me here."

All five of them stood in a loose circle, mostly looking at the ground, but Lorica and Mattis watched each other. She wore a puzzled look, as if she were doing a really hard math problem in her head. "We can make it better for each other," she said to the group, but she was really speaking to Mattis. Mattis wore a puzzled look, too, as if he were doing an easy math problem, but one that was still beyond him. "We can work together, I think, to make—"

She stopped speaking as the door slid open. AG bounded out, clanking his limbs against his torso in his excitement and rush to get out of the comms center. "Gang!" AG hollered. "You gotta hear—Hey!" He stopped short when he saw Lorica. She scowled first at Mattis, then at Dec and

AG. Her teeth were bared. "You *keetar freg*," she seethed. Mattis didn't know what that meant but could tell it was a nasty Zeltron epithet. She shoved Dec. He fell backward into AG, and they both rattled to the ground. "You tricked me," she said. "You used me because you were sneaking around in there. You made me—" She couldn't finish the sentence. She started away, then turned back to face Mattis.

He gasped for air. He hadn't used her. He wasn't just saying those things to distract her from discovering their troublemaking. He'd really felt them, felt his heart and mind open up. He'd spoken honestly. It hurt him that she felt tricked, because he knew she'd been honest, too. But it didn't matter. There was nothing he could say. Lorica swung a swift fist in his direction, but in the moment before it made contact, she changed her mind, opened her palm, and lowered it so she gave him a hard cuff in the chest instead, grunting as she did. The air went out of Mattis's lungs, and he doubled over. When he looked up again, Lorica was storming off in the direction of her barracks.

Sari helped Dec and AG-90 to their feet. Klimo patted Mattis on the back. "You okay, friend?" he asked. Mattis shook his head. He wasn't okay.

The security door slid open again. What else could possibly go wrong?

Jo Jerjerrod stepped out of the comms center and directly into their group. His face fell.

"You screwups," he sneered. "You were spying on me."

"Technically, only Aygee was spying on you," Dec said unhelpfully.

Jo swiveled his head to look at the droid, and AG had to take a step back, so sharp was their squad leader's glare.

"I didn't—" AG started, but it didn't matter. Jo had turned a deep red; a vein in his neck throbbed like a snake under a tarp.

Mattis was too afraid, not to mention too tired, too embarrassed, and too upset about Lorica, to do much of anything. If Dec and AG wanted to wriggle out of this one, they were on their own. And Mattis believed they'd do it. Dec always got away with everything. Jo might get mad, but there was little he could do to Dec if he wasn't allowed to boot him from the Resistance altogether.

Or maybe Mattis was wrong. Jo grabbed AG by the arm and pulled the droid close to him. "Come with me," he said.

"Careful, chief. That arm's been around; it'll come right off in your hand," AG complained.

Jo reached into his pocket for a comlink and said, "Security droids, report to comms center four. Some recruits need an escort back to their bunks."

"You'll want to let go of my brother," Dec said evenly.

"I got this, Dec," AG said. "Jo, we need to talk about what happened in there."

"No we do not," Jo said. His voice was hard. His teeth were clenched.

"Take your doshin' hands off," Dec said with a mean smile.

Sari took a step forward to help AG. Jo warned her off with a look, but it didn't work; she took another step. Jo was about to say something else, something certainly menacing, but the sentry droids arrived and did his talking for him. Mattis hadn't even heard them hum up to the group. They spoke in unison: *"Return to your barracks."*

"What are you doing?" Mattis asked. He choked on the words, and no one heard him. He cleared his throat and said again, "What are you doing with Aygee, Jo?"

Jo finally noticed Mattis, but all he did was

echo the droids. "Return to your barracks." He snorted and dragged AG away from them. The sentry droids circled in front of Jo and AG. Cutting off the rest of the group.

"You let my brother loose, Jo, or I'm gonna— I'll . . . I will *throw* one of these droids at you."

Mattis didn't know what to do. He felt light-headed, like all of space was zooming in on him. "Jo," he said. "Where are you taking Aygee?"

AG struggled against Jo's grip, but Jo didn't relent. "I'm gonna wipe this droid," he said. "Make a soldier out of him, since I can't make one of the rest of you. Maybe then you'll learn something." And with that, Jo turned and dragged AG along with him, heading toward the droid maintenance site.

Dec roared and charged after them. One of the sentries ejected a small electro-prod from its chassis. As Dec tried to bust through the droids, it pulsed him with a quick shock. Dec was thrown back. All Mattis remembered after that was flailing after Dec as he took another run for his brother, the sound of another pulse, and then darkness.

CHAPTER
06

MATTIS WOKE UP SLOWLY. Klimo's hot breath filled Mattis's nose, and the bumps of his skin grazed Mattis's face. The Rodian was watching him *very* closely, which was only slightly more unnerving than not remembering how he'd gotten back to his bunk.

"Oh, good, you're awake!" Klimo shouted. "Now go to sleep. We are going to be in so much trouble tomorrow. You'll need your sleep! Jo will make us do oh so many push-ups. My arms will probably fall off. Too bad about those Hubbard pies, but oh well. Good night." He hopped down and into his bunk.

Mattis lowered himself to the ground slowly to

see if everything still worked. It did, but everything was sore. He put his boots on gingerly. "Best friend?" Klimo murmured from under his covers.

"I can't let him wipe Aygee." Mattis realized his conviction as he said it.

"What can we do? There's a sentry outside our door, Jo's our squad leader, and . . ." Klimo trailed off.

"And?" Mattis pushed.

"We're just us." Klimo sighed. "I want to save him, too. Aygee is funny and nice to me, but I'm just me and you're just you. What can we do?"

Mattis had never thought of himself as *just* anyone. He was a hero. His parents were heroes. He'd taught kids at the orphan farm to stand up to bullies. He'd stood up to bullies himself. He wasn't a "just." He thought of the time he'd beaten Fikk on Durkteel. He showed that bully a . . . Wait. Mattis realized that he hadn't beaten Fikk. He hadn't shown that bully anything. He had *escaped* Fikk. He'd bravely *run away*. He'd looked danger in the eye a few times and hadn't flinched, but neither had danger. Well, this time he was going to stand up. This was for AG. "I'll show you what we can do, just us," Mattis answered Klimo. "Come on."

Mattis opened the door and found himself face to face with a sentry droid. His skin itched, remembering the shock he'd gotten—however long before that had happened.

"Please return to your quarters," the droid said in a monotone, opening the compartment that held the electro-prod.

Klimo whimpered and tugged at Mattis's sleeve. "We're just us."

"Please return to your quarters," the droid repeated.

Mattis thought of AG speaking in a monotone like that. AG in droid-face, with no alternative. *No,* Mattis thought. *No doshin' way.* He was thinking like Dec, which was good, because Dec could have talked his way past the droid, and that's what Mattis needed to do.

"Hey, droid," Mattis said, drawling a very little bit. He realized what Dec might have done, and he was going to give it a try. "Your directive was to, what? See us to our quarters? Keep us here?"

"Affirmative." The droid didn't sound suspicious of Mattis, but only because suspicion was outside of its programming.

"Well, you did it! We were kept here for—I don't know how long, because I got zapped. Klimo? How long have we been kept here?"

"Thirteen epicycles, best friend!" Mattis didn't know how long that was, because Klimo never stopped using Rodian measures of time, but it didn't matter.

"So. You have achieved your directive," Mattis said, clapping his hands onto the droid's shoulders like he was congratulating it. "Would you like a new directive? I've got one for you. Here it is. Escort us to droid maintenance. Right. Doshing. Now."

Klimo smiled as well as a Rodian could.

Mattis felt pretty good about himself until the droid responded: "Negative."

"What?" Mattis cried.

"The directive is incomplete. The directive is to keep you here until morning. It is not morning. Directive incomplete. Return to your quarters or be returned to your quarters. Please comply."

Mattis commanded the version of Dec that had set up camp in his brain to think of something else. He was about ready to throw Klimo at the robot.

"I wish we could amend the directive," Klimo

said with a sigh, accidentally saving the day.

"Klimo, that's it!" Jo may have given the droid its directive, but although he was squad leader, Jo didn't hold official technical rank over his squad, not as far as ordering droids was concerned. They were all cadets, and though the higher-ups might trust Jo more, and though the squad was supposed to follow his orders, to an automaton, all cadets were ranked equally. Including Mattis. "Amend directive," Mattis commanded in a strong voice.

"Please enter amended directive."

"Keep us in our quarters until . . . what do you think, Klimo?" Mattis asked.

"Ten micro-epicycles from now!"

"In Basic, Klimo."

"Thirty seconds, best friend!"

"Thirty seconds then," Mattis ordered the robot. Exactly thirty seconds later, the droid retracted the electro-prod and scooted away to engage in its automatic directives.

Mattis and Klimo snuck through the corridors toward droid maintenance. It felt like a mission. Mattis and Klimo watched each other's backs, and their assignment was to avoid detection and save an ally. Klimo's antennae twitched, and he pushed Mattis back into a shadow. "Someone's coming!" He didn't quite manage to whisper, but it was closer than usual.

"Klimo?" Sari popped her head around the corner.

Mattis shushed Klimo before he could yell. He waved Sari over.

Sari asked if he was feeling all right. "You took quite a shock," she said. He shrugged. She continued, "Jo posted sentry droids at all our doors. How did you get past yours?"

"Amended its orders. Klimo's idea," Mattis said. Klimo blushed a pale blue.

Sari beamed. "Good one. I came up with an override code. I'll have to show you sometime."

"Those will both work, but in a pinch, you can always pour a cup of water on its head," Dec said, appearing out of nowhere. "Sentries can take the cold vacuum of space but a cup of water? No. They tried 'em on Ques. Didn't last two seconds. Humidity in the air took 'em right out. Couldn't even use 'em for parts. Now come on. Let's go get my brother."

They went in a small clutch, pausing at each forbidden door while Sari sliced them through.

Dec got increasingly anxious each time. As Sari crouched and fiddled with the final security lock, Mattis told Dec, "Try to stay . . ." He was going to say "calm," but looking at Dec's rage-streaked face, Mattis didn't think that would be possible. "Don't punch Jo," he said instead.

"No promises."

The door to the droid maintenance site slid open, and the four of them crowded through the doorway. It was dark in there. A few sparks flew in a shadowy corner, illuminating the room for moments at a time. Soft bleeps and bloops of either droids working or droids being worked on filled the air. The room had the aspect of a repair shop crossed with a mortuary.

Metal tables like slabs, cluttered with robot parts and maintenance tools, filled the room. So strewn with detritus was the site that Mattis didn't see the G2 repair droid standing on a high chair, tinkering away on a prone chassis. They apparently took the G2 by surprise, as well.

"Oh, hello!" it yelled, its eyes lighting up and its servos whirring. "It's you! Who are you? I am Geetoo-Peeeye. I was just working. You don't work here, do you? I'd recognize you."

"We don't," Mattis said, scanning the room.

"We're looking for a droid," Dec told G2-PI.

PI swiveled his head in a circle, then steadied it with his hands. "Whoo! Dizzying. Well," he said. "Not me, I expect. And I don't know anyone here. But I'd love to. Who are you again? This is a restricted area."

"Anybody have a cup of water?" Dec asked.

Sari stepped forward, and for a second, Mattis thought she was going to punch or reprogram the G2, but there were more than two ways to slice a droid. "I'm Sari," she said. "And this is Klimo. I don't think you two have met."

Klimo leaped forward with his arms outstretched. "Hello!" he cried.

"Hello!" PI echoed.

"Your work looks very interesting," Klimo started in.

"Oh, it is!" the repair droid said, excited that anyone would want to talk about his boring, boring efforts.

Klimo's natural enthusiasm and the G2 model's innate gabbiness would serve as a perfect distraction for the rest of them to quickly search the overcrowded maintenance site.

They spread out, but they didn't have to go far. Behind a row of disused robot pieces,

Mattis—then Dec, then Sari—nearly stumbled on Jo and Lorica. Jo growled an indecipherable order to another G2 unit. Lorica said something, but her words were drowned out by the G2's firing up an impact wrench. The G2's eyes glowed, illuminating its workspace and revealing AG-90. AG was facedown on a slab. He was completely powered down. Mattis had never seen something so animated, so resounding with the stuff of life, rendered so completely defunct. It was jarring. There wasn't even a word for the way AG's shell seemed. It was as if it had never contained spirit at all.

"No!" Dec pounced on Jo, who deflected Dec's blow at the last moment. They both went to the ground, crashing through the junk piled up on the floor.

While they scrapped, Mattis and Sari hurried to AG's side.

"Turn him back on!" Mattis demanded, not sure if he was talking to the G2 droid or Lorica. "What did you do?"

"We're too late," Sari sobbed.

Lorica shook her head—was she telling Mattis that they still had time or was she just disappointed in him?—and turned to join the fray with

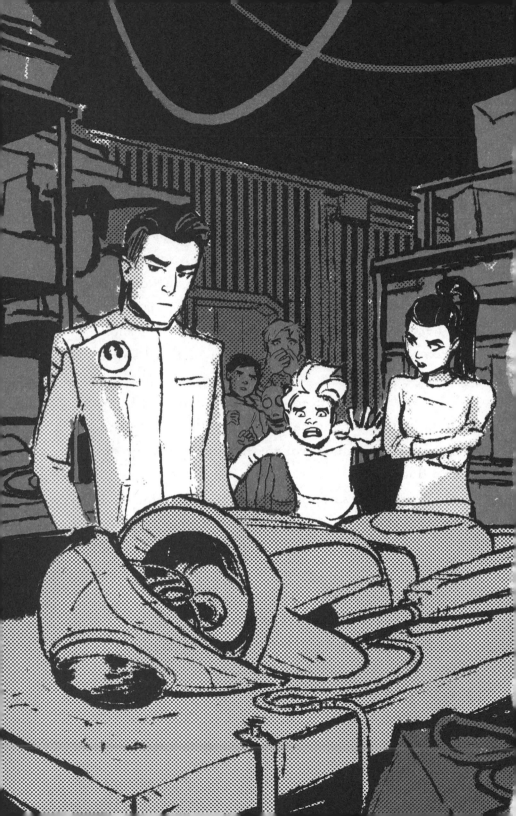

Dec and Jo. She pulled Dec off, but he kicked, thumping Jo square in the chest. Jo went back down, and Lorica whirled with Dec, tossing him into another pile of debris.

"Sari, help him," Mattis said, almost offhandedly. He braced the repair droid, grabbing it by its shoulder joints. "Stop whatever you're doing," he ordered.

The G2's eye-lights blinked out. This one was not garrulous and chummy like the one they'd left with Klimo. It happened sometimes: a droid that took too much pleasure in taking apart its fellow droids. Mattis could tell at once that this G2 was one of those.

"I have my orders," the G2 said, jerking its mechanical hand back at Jo.

"Ignore your orders!" Mattis felt something—the Force?—swell inside him. He wouldn't allow harm to come to his friend.

"I would," the G2 sneered, "but the current is already running." It held up a pair of cables that were wired to AG's insides. The other ends disappeared into a control panel in the room's wall. The G2 droid made burbling noises that were meant to emulate a cackle.

"Dec," Mattis called, desperate, not knowing what to do.

Dec stopped struggling against Lorica.

"It's already happening," Mattis told him. "There's no way to shut it down."

Dec roared again as something primal erupted within him. "Sari," he shouted. "Get them away from me."

Sari grabbed Lorica, picking her up in a hug. Lorica kicked and wriggled to free herself, swearing in both Basic and Zeltron, as if that would help.

Dec looked around desperately. Finally, his eyes fell on a corner of the room, toward the ceiling. The incident power switch-off: a hard-to-reach toggle placed in every command room in case of emergency. Every building, every light, every computer would be shut down. It was meant to be used only in a kay-one-zero base abandonment scenario.

"Heck with it," Dec said.

He bolted for the switch-off, and Jo ran to intercept him. If Jo was successful, AG's memory would be wiped. Mattis's first friend on the base, Dec's brother, would be gone. But if Dec shut down the base, they would surely be expelled from the Resistance. Not to mention the other trouble they might cause. What if they were attacked? Any base shields would be gone if Dec turned off the power.

Those moral calculations took place in Mattis's head in a split second, and he decided there was no decision to make at all. As Jo lunged for the sprinting Dec, Mattis leaped out at Jo and tackled him to the ground. He was only successful because he had surprise on his side; Mattis could never have taken Jo down in a fair fight. But there was nothing fair about any of this.

Dec tore for the corner. Sari, seeing how high the toggle was, tossed Lorica aside, and fell into step behind Dec. As they reached the corner, Sari lowered her hands like a platform. Dec stepped on, Sari raised him up, and he punched the toggle.

The result was immediate. The lights in the maintenance site blinked out, plunging them all into darkness. The only light came from the eyes of the various droids that surrounded them. All over the base, they heard lights, computers, generators, and machinery shutting down or grinding to an unintended halt. Voices came next. There were muffled shouts from the corridors and echoes of people calling out in confusion across the base.

In the dark, Dec scrambled to AG's side, knocking over tools and parts of other droids. He switched his brother back on and turned him over. A whirring noise, followed by a thick clanking, filled the dark. In the shine of the maintenance droid's eye-lights, AG sat up. Had they succeeded? Had they cut the power in time?

They waited. One tense, silent moment ticked by, then another. AG just sat on the slab table. He was still. He was quiet.

Dec whispered, "Aygee? Brother?"

AG swiveled his head stiffly. In the powerless silence, they could hear the lenses in his eyes dilate.

The G2 that had been servicing AG pointed at each of them. "You're all going to be in a great deal of tr—" AG shoved the droid off its high stool.

AG clicked the lens of his right eye shut and back open, winking. He held his left hand over his right and wiggled his thumb.

Dec sighed in relief.

"Aygee-Ninety, you had me worried!" Dec exclaimed, slapping his brother's back.

AG replied with a series of beeps and whistles.

He sounded like an R2 unit. Everyone was completely surprised, but none more than AG himself. He pointed at Jo and chirped angrily.

"You altered his language settings?" Dec demanded.

"Worry about yourselves. You really are in trouble," Jo began. "All of you. This isn't some sort of—"

Mattis didn't know why Jo stopped talking until he heard what Jo must have. Incoming. An attack? Now? J-Squadron may have doomed them all.

"I got Aygee," Sari said, hoisting the droid over her shoulder. She was first out of the maintenance center, with the others right behind.

When they got outside, they realized they weren't in danger, just trouble. So much trouble. Ships were incoming, but it wasn't an attack. It was the X-wing squadron back from its extended mission. The pilots were coming in for a landing on a tarmac that was pitch-black.

Mattis, Dec, Sari, AG, Klimo, Lorica, and Jo huddled outside the command center, watching the red and white lights of the X-wings veer dangerously close to each other, their pilots undoubtedly trying to gauge where the night sky ended and the landing strip began. Their astromechs' navicomputers couldn't help them. The Resistance base was a dead zone when it came to technology. The lead X-wing swooped down at too high a speed, then abruptly pulled up, the tail of the ship smashing over some ground equipment. The other fighters followed suit, heading back into the sky.

They'd find a way to land, Mattis was sure. They had to. They were expert flyers, the best of the best. They'd figure it out.

Mattis believed everything would be okay, hoped the pilots would know what to do, but Jo took action. He called each of their names and threw them emergency flares. The ground crew passed them out with determination and speed. Everyone on the base worked together to guide the pilots to the ground safely.

Mattis was determined to help. He stole only one look at Jo, whose expression reinforced what Mattis knew to be true: once everyone was safely back on base and the power was restored, Mattis and his friends would face punishment for what they'd done.

CHAPTER

07

KLIMO WAS BOUNCING so fast that he shook the entire bench. Mattis, Dec, and Sari sat with him, and his energy felt like an insistent, impatient pulse. Like a tribal Ewok drumbeat heralding some terrible event. *That isn't much of an exaggeration,* Mattis thought. A terrible event was both behind and ahead of them, the former of their own doing and the latter at the hands of Admiral Ackbar.

The Resistance leader was shaking with frustration. The whole room seemed to be minutely convulsing with the pent-up energy they were each sending off. Even Lorica didn't know what to do with her hands. She fidgeted as if sending signals then finally put them in her pockets. Standing between her and AG, Jo stared coolly ahead, tapping his foot to some unheard rhythm.

It hadn't taken the Resistance leadership long to discover who had activated the incident power switch-off. The group had been immediately separated and held in different rooms that felt like prison cells. It seemed as if they were being quarantined to keep them from agreeing on a reasonable story, but to Mattis, the most reasonable story was the truth: AG had seen Jo do something he wasn't supposed to in that communications center, so Jo had tried to wipe AG's memory. Jo could pretend all he wanted that he was attempting to make AG a better soldier. The truth was, Jo was covering something up.

Unfortunately, AG hadn't yet been able to tell them what he'd witnessed. The commanders who'd spoken—sternly—with each of them didn't seem to care what Jo had done, only that a calamitous breaking of rules had transpired. They'd told Mattis to "leave Jo Jerjerrod to Ackbar, per the admiral's orders." Mattis accepted that, but he hadn't yet seen Admiral Ackbar confront Jo about breaking into the communications center. Mattis was only seeing Admiral Ackbar now, as he yelled at them all. It didn't seem like the appropriate time or place for AG to catch them up.

"You could have killed an entire squadron of fighters!" Admiral Ackbar shouted, throwing his hands in the air in exasperation.

None of them spoke.

"You got lucky," Ackbar continued. "Due to quick thinking, there wasn't much damage and, thank the Force, no loss of life, but that does not mean there won't be consequences! There *will* be consequences!" He banged on a table. "I'm sending you away," he said, more softly.

Mattis felt like he had been struck. They were being kicked out of the Resistance. He'd finally found a home, and he was being expelled from it. He felt like the floor had disappeared under him, like he was free-falling. He couldn't catch his breath. Stars appeared in the periphery of his vision.

Dec's hand on his shoulder brought him back to land. The stars fell away, and the room was clear and quiet again. Each of them looked gut-punched. The room had an airless quality. Every sound was muted.

Admiral Ackbar cocked his head at Mattis like he was an oddity. "Mattis. You were breathing funny, son."

Mattis looked up at Admiral Ackbar, his hero. He nodded because he was afraid that if he tried to speak, he would cry.

"This is a punishment," he said. "But it's still a mission. Make no mistake about that. I'm sending you to Vodran."

A mission? Vodran? They weren't being kicked out? Mattis couldn't help smiling in relief.

Admiral Ackbar shook his head. "No. No smiles," he said. "Vodran is a terrible place. It's murky; it's dank. It was the stronghold of Harra the Hutt. She and her collection of scum and troublemakers abandoned Vodran during an Imperial incursion, and as far as we know, the settlements were reduced to rubble by the Empire years ago. The swamp has taken back most of the planet." Admiral Ackbar pushed some buttons on his console and a holomap was projected above them. "It's fetid and unfit for civilized life. It's bogs and muck. So no smiles."

He twiddled some dials on his console, and image after image of buildings turned to wreckage appeared. What remained of them was choked with black-and-green overgrowth. Mattis felt like he could smell the planet's wretched stench from the images alone.

"The rest of J-Squad will be disbanded and incorporated into other units. You are going to Vodran, and you're going to scrounge for usable weaponry, vehicles, and parts. Anything that might be useful to the Resistance. You'll stay there for as long as it takes. While you're there, maybe you can learn to work together as a team. Maybe you can prove yourselves useful to and worthy of the Resistance. I do believe in all of you. But hear me clearly: you all have a lot of trouble to dig yourselves out of. Grab your shovels. You're going to need them."

CHAPTER

08

AN ANCIENT CARGO ship, too cavernous for its load of two short-range transports and seven young Resistance recruits, took them to the Si'Klaata Cluster. Even the black space around those planets felt filthy to Mattis. They could see Vodran through their viewports. A weak green light glowed through a murky fog of burnt-toast-colored cloud cover. They boarded the two short-range transports: Mattis, Dec, and Klimo in one; Jo, Lorica, Sari, and AG in the other. It didn't escape anyone's notice that Jo kept AG close to him and sequestered from the rest of them. Dec seemed to be biding his time for a confrontation.

The transports carried them to Vodran, the cargo ship growing small in the distance. At a certain point, it would leave the cluster and return to the Resistance base. It would return periodically so J-Squadron could retrieve supplies, but they were otherwise alone. They'd be making camp in the muck of Vodran, pitching tents and attempting to build fires in the fetid swamplands.

As bad as it was, Mattis was excited for one aspect of the detail: speeder bikes. There was too much marsh to go very far on foot, so they'd been issued some extremely used speeders. Mattis didn't care about the dings or dents or sputtering engines. Mattis's favorite training exercise had been on those speeders. No matter how lousy of a detail it was supposed to be, he was going to get to open up a speeder bike's throttle to see how fast he could go. Each bike had a detector strapped to it to locate inorganic objects in the swamp or in the brush that had overtaken the buildings.

Dec landed his transport on nearly solid land. The ship sank slightly into the ground. They set down in distant sight of what used to be Harra the Hutt's stronghold. They were meant to sweep the intervening landscape, day by day, scavenging for usable gear. They would load whatever they found onto the transports and take it all to the stronghold. The Resistance would send a larger ship there to transfer the salvaged junk off-planet. But that was days, maybe weeks, away. For the time being, that mud-sunk quagmire was their home.

Dec stepped off the transport ship, his boot sinking into the sludge. "Swamp, sweet swamp," he said, grinning.

Lorica, deboarding the other transport, glared at him.

Dec called over, "It really is like comin' home, ain't it?" AG nodded and whistled.

Mattis didn't think they were funny. "You're not funny," he said.

Dec sloughed through some more mud. "We're not being funny. This isn't far from our home planet, and Ques looks a lot like this. Only . . . on Ques there's more domiciles sticking out of the mud."

AG joined them in the muck. "And, y'know, people," Dec continued, moving in closer to AG.

"It *is* like home! Taste that air!" Klimo yelled.

Dec told AG, "We gotta talk."

AG chirruped cryptically. Dec shook his head, lost.

"Anybody understand this beeping droid language?" Dec asked the group.

Jo was on them immediately. He hovered on his speeder bike. "I do. Now form a line." Jo ordered them to spend the day scavenging in one direction, with several meters between them. They would encounter grasping, overgrown plant life. He warned them to be wary of dianogas. The one-eyed cephalopods were indigenous to Vodran and probably hungry. Jo didn't want any of his charges being eaten; it would reflect poorly on him.

"Nice to know you care," Lorica said. Mattis was surprised to hear her snap back. She must be really angry about being there.

They spread out as ordered and began cruising over the marshes. Klimo cheered. He loved the speeder bike drills even more than Mattis did. Sari wobbled uneasily, too big for her bike. For Dec and AG, it was old hat. Lorica kept her distance from the rest of them. Mattis took off, and for just a moment, he felt like he had in his dream the night before leaving Durkteel, like he had Admiral Ackbar commanding him and he was taking on the whole Empire.

"Mattis!" Jo snapped him back to reality. "Ride

with your eyes open! That's rule one. Rule two is to stay in sight of the others. You know how fast you were going? You ride this bike into a tree, and you better not survive. It's worth more to the Resistance than you are."

Mattis tried to think of something cutting to say back, but Jo wasn't interested. He was already riding away and into formation. Jo yelled back, "Prove me wrong," as if there was no way Mattis ever could.

They scanned the swamp, occasionally dipping in to retrieve a piece of a ship or building. They kept mechanical items and left structural ones. Occasionally, a hill would emerge from the mire like a breaching beast, and one or another of them would be able to scan dry land. But mostly they were in dank swampland. A canopy of gnarled, foreboding trees blocked out any brightness Vodran's covering of brown clouds allowed. As they moved deeper into it, the vegetation clustered closer and intertwined; woody limbs hooked woody limbs, and low trees bent their spires together as if whispering wet secrets. It was slow going.

———

It wasn't long before Lorica on one end and Klimo on the other had disappeared behind brush. Jo split off after Lorica and told AG to find Klimo and bring him back. The group needed to stay in formation. Mattis figured Jo didn't want to leave AG with any of the rest of them.

As soon as they lost visual contact with Jo, Mattis and Dec veered off after AG, who was waiting for them. Sari had strayed a bit beyond them. She was at the foot of a tall twisted tree, staring into its great umbrella of foliage. They couldn't get her attention, so they got off their bikes and went over to her.

"What are you looking at?" Mattis asked her.

"Birds," she said distractedly. "I love birds."

"Me too," Mattis said, scanning for the birds she saw. "Anything that flies, I like."

"All the variety of life in the universe in just one species." Mattis wasn't exactly sure what Sari meant by that, but she clearly meant to mean something, so he just nodded solemnly.

Mattis told Sari about his big book of birds at the base and said he'd loan it to her if they made it back. She had two to swap with him. Finally, Mattis saw the birds she was looking at. Tufted cackys. Four of them, in multi-hues of brown to

camouflage themselves but with bright pink spots on their chests. Now that he saw them, he couldn't believe he'd ever missed them. They were splashes of brightness in the muck. They were a family. The parents were showing the babies how to fly.

"Can we break up this tea party? I didn't bring no scones," Dec drawled. "Lookit that, Aygee. Your works're gonna get muddied something awful." He shook himself down a bit, spraying wet grit everywhere.

Dec took a tool out of his boot and popped AG's chest open, working quickly. "Let me know when you can talk right again."

"Maybe it isn't so bad, what he saw," Sari offered.

"Maybe there's an explanation." Mattis hoped that was true.

"Then why am I trying to restore Aygee's language setting? Why'd Jo put a clamp on it?"

"You want me to try?" Sari offered. "I'm good with clamps."

"He's *my* brother, dosh it!" Dec growled. He softened. "Sorry."

"I understand," Sari said, and scanned the surroundings for Jo.

Dec pulled another tool out of his boot. It

sounded to Mattis like he was scraping at something inside AG. "Almost got it . . . Just . . . just a little bit more . . .

"Got it!" yelled Dec, and with a cracking sound so loud it set the tufted cackys squawking angrily, he popped a restrainer bolt out of his brother's chest and into the swamp, where it sank. "Aw, I was gonna shove that down Jo's throat," Dec said in disappointment.

"Much better," sighed AG, closing his own chest plate. "I've had so much bottled up. First of all, in case this happens again, Dec, you need to learn beeping language. Second, for units that talk too danged much, G2's sure ain't got nothin' to say. That's what I meant when I pushed that G2 off me. Been holding on to that for a while."

"Yeah, yeah. What did you see? What's Jo's secret?" Dec asked, replacing his tools in his boot.

AG couldn't meet Dec's eye. "You're better off not knowing. He stole language from me. Who knows what he'd do to the rest of you?"

Dec spat. "If Jo's up to no good, it's no use keepin' his secret. If the Resistance doesn't see that we're on the right side of things and Jo ain't, then I don't want to be a part of the Resistance.

Tell us what you saw and let's handle it, or else what good is it that we're each other's people?"

AG looked from Dec to Sari to Mattis. It was as if he'd read instructions on his friends' faces. They were there for each other. He had to tell them the truth. Behind him, the family of birds flew away together. Mattis and Sari couldn't help smiling.

"All right," AG said. They leaned in, and the droid started telling them what they were so eager to hear. "Jo Jerjerrod is—"

AG didn't get to finish, because that was when the dianoga took him.

CHAPTER

09

A DIANOGA WAS ROUGHLY the size of a large dinner table. Its body was generally submerged underwater, so only its single eyestalk was visible, but somehow this cephalopod had flopped itself onto the squishy hummock on which the group had paused. A dianoga possessed seven suckered tentacles, two of which wrapped around AG-90's torso and started to drag him into deeper swamp. They could hear the gnashing of the spiked teeth that surrounded its pulsating maw.

"It's chewing on my foot! Get the danged thing off!" AG howled before his voice processor got jammed into the dreck.

Mattis grabbed hold of AG's upper arm. The

dianoga pulled hard and made high-pitched squelching sounds. Mattis feared he'd pull AG's arm off. He wasn't strong enough to free the droid.

"Sari," he said, snapping her to attention. "Grab his torso."

She was on AG in a moment, flopping down in the mud and hugging him around the middle while the dianoga squalled and shook the droid. Dec batted at the creature with a chunk of wood, and the dianoga simultaneously pulled AG off the mound toward subaqueous wetland and slapped away Dec's attacks. The creature went into a slippery roll, turning AG over and over, but Sari didn't let go. The dianoga was strong. They needed a new tactic.

"Sari, can you get this thing off of him?" Mattis shouted.

"Can't do that and hold AG at the same time," she yelled back.

AG lifted his head from the muck. "Keep holding me!" he cried.

Mattis got into a crouch and launched himself at AG, grabbing him around the waist beside Sari. "Okay," he huffed. "I can try to hold him here. You get the thing off."

Sari hauled herself up. Sheets of mud dropped from her body. Dec hacked again at the dianoga with his piece of wood; he had no effect. It snatched him with another of its tentacles and pulled him into the mud toward its puckering mouth.

For someone who didn't like to be the team muscle, Sari sure knew how to fill that role when it counted. She roared like something wild and pressed her body into the rot-stinking dianoga. She lifted it high, and it squealed and gnashed. It dropped Dec but still clung to AG.

Sari squeezed the creature tight. It didn't like that at all. It wailed a high-pitched complaint. Dec and Mattis worked the tentacles until they finally pried them off AG.

"I'm out!" AG shouted. Sari let go. The dianoga splashed down and swam away.

Dec lifted his face out of the viscous guck. "You were telling us something?"

Mattis rolled AG onto his back. The droid was banged up but functional. His eyes flashed a couple of times, and he lifted himself to a sitting position. "Yeah," AG said. "Jo Jerjerrod is a traitor."

CHAPTER

10

WHEN THE SECURITY door had slid closed, separating AG from his friends, he had found himself in darkness. He stopped moving. He didn't want to make any noise. He dimmed his eye-lights. He was at the end of the long corridor, and he shuffled quietly toward the one room with lights on.

He heard muffled voices even before he reached the open door. AG peered inside.

Jo sat hunched forward, intensely listening to the man and woman on the holo-comm. They were both middle-aged. The man's face was drawn and serious. His hair was cut short like Jo's. The woman looked vaguely amused. She nodded when she spoke.

"Great progress has been made, Jo," she said. "We have the location of a map that will lead us to Luke Skywalker. Finding Skywalker will change the course of things."

AG wasn't certain exactly what was happening. He knew the Resistance was looking for Luke Skywalker, so maybe those people were on a mission for General Organa? But why report to Jo? Why didn't J-Squadron know about Jo's mission?

It wasn't until the conversation had continued a bit and the man stood up for a moment that AG comprehended what was happening. The man wore a military uniform, slate gray and severe-looking. It wasn't a uniform AG-90 had seen on any Resistance personnel, and he was fairly certain the insignia on the chest didn't represent anyone in the New Republic.

Which could only mean one thing . . .

The woman spoke: "Jo, the Supreme Leader believes in tradition. He, and everyone here, believes in greatness passed through generations. You come from a long line of loyal warriors who have tried and succeeded in changing the order of the galaxy. When you come home to us, Jo, you shall join your rightful place in the First Order."

Hearing the story from AG, in the swamps

of Vodran, Mattis was physically revolted. He doubled over and put his hands on his knees, trying to catch his breath. Jo was sneaking around at night, making secret holo-calls to First Order military personnel? Jo was a jerk, but Mattis hadn't thought he could be a traitor.

"I knew it," Dec said.

"You did not." AG waved him away.

"Well, I knew something was up with Jo. He's so strict and by the book, y'know? No one acts that way unless they're overcompensating for being a double-crosser."

"I can't believe it," Sari said.

"We have to tell Admiral Ackbar," Mattis said, but he was disappointed. Jo was far from a friend, but he was someone Mattis had admired. It had always seemed to Mattis that Jo wanted to do good.

How could a person betray the Resistance? How could someone see what General Organa and Admiral Ackbar and the others were doing, as Jo had taken Mattis to see that first day, and then decide to stab them in their backs? Those people, their leaders, were heroes. History had proven that.

"There are comms on the transports," Sari reminded them.

They got on their bikes and sped solemnly back the way they had come.

They went over the last hummock, and the transport ships came into view. So did Lorica, who stood on the boarding ramp of one of the ships with her boot in her hand. She was scraping it on the edge of the ramp. They parked their bikes and walked toward the ship.

"There's muck on my boot," she told them as they approached.

"I know how it feels," Dec said.

Lorica stopped scraping and glared at them. She pulled her boot back on. "You're not supposed to be on the ships. None of us are. I'm not even supposed to be here, which is why I'm about to bike back out onto this garbage planet and look for, I don't know, some half-deteriorated Y-wing." She shook her head, focusing. "Anyway, you'll get in more trouble."

"We couldn't possibly get in more trouble," Sari countered.

"You'll get *me* in more trouble, I mean," Lorica clarified.

Dec sneered. "We have to contact the base. You wouldn't understand."

"I understand a lot," she said. The statement seemed loaded with meaning.

"Can you just trust us?" Mattis asked.

Lorica barked a laugh.

Mattis tried complete honesty. "Jo is a traitor."

Lorica shook her head. "What are you talking about?"

"Aygee saw him," Mattis said.

"How do you know? Wait, you fixed him?" Lorica asked Sari.

"Dec did," AG said.

"Good. That wasn't right, what Jo did, but that doesn't make him a traitor. What if you're wrong?" she asked AG.

"I ain't."

"But what if you are?"

"I ain't."

"Can you allow for the possibility?"

AG considered that. "Naw," he said.

"Permission to board?" Dec said wryly as he, AG, and Sari headed up the boarding ramp and inside. Lorica grabbed Mattis by the arm. He felt that same floating-and-sinking sensation in his gut, like he might cry or laugh or do both.

"Mattis, make sense for a second." She was

grave. "If you take this to Ackbar and you're wrong—you can't just run around the Resistance base yelling 'traitor.' People like Ackbar take that really seriously."

"It is serious," Mattis countered.

"But if you're wrong . . . you've made accusations. You've thrown things into upset. You could be in more trouble than you are now. I don't think there's any coming back from this accusation. You could get us all kicked out."

"Aygee isn't wrong," Mattis said, though a bit uncertainly. "He can't be."

"He *could* be," she reasoned. "Maybe Jo's doing something for General Organa. Who knows? Jo wouldn't betray the Resistance. Jo *loves* the Resistance." She didn't let go of his arm, but she softened her grip. "You understand that, Mattis. He needs the Resistance just like you do. Just like I do."

Mattis's head dropped. She had that effect on him. She weakened his resolve every time. It was because he knew she was smarter and more accomplished than he was. He trusted Lorica, despite the fact that she didn't seem to like him very much. Maybe he trusted her *because* of that.

He wished having the Force meant he could resist her sway.

"I'll get them to talk to Jo first," he said.

"Good enough," she agreed.

Mattis hurried into the ship. He made his case with the others. They knew what AG had seen. They owed it to Jo to hear him out. Dec waved that away, but Mattis insisted. If Jo hadn't judged Dec and AG instantly and regarded them as trouble, if he hadn't decided that Sari was just muscle, wouldn't they all have been better off? Wouldn't they have been a more cohesive unit? Well, there they were, judging Jo just as rashly. They owed it to him to confront him and find out if there was any explanation. Mattis promised Dec that he could punch Jo really hard if they were right. Dec agreed to those terms, and moments later, they were all, including Lorica, biking through the swamp to confront Jo.

CHAPTER

11

T HEY FOUND JO in a clearing on a sur-
prisingly lush piece of dry land, staring out
into distant space. They got off their bikes.
Mattis felt as if he were intruding. But this wasn't
Jo's home or secret sanctum. He had received the
same punishment they all had. Based on what AG
had told them, he should receive even more. So
why was Mattis unsure, all of a sudden?

Dec obviously had no such pause in his con-
victions. He marched up to Jo and cuffed him on
his shoulder. "Finding it hard to do your dirty
work out here, chief?"

"It's all dirty work out here," Jo said, sighing.

Dec was taken aback. "Did you—I'm sorry, did
you just make a joke?"

Lorica told Jo, "This may not be the best time for jokes."

Dec said, "Aw, don't dash his dreams, Lor. It's his first joke!"

"Don't call me Lor," she snapped at Dec.

"Why aren't you all scavenging?" Jo asked, shaking off whatever reverie he'd been in.

"'Cause we gotta talk to you," Dec said. He poked Jo in the chest.

"Knock it off, Hansen. Get back out into the bog."

Mattis and Sari stood slightly apart from the others. Sari was peering up at the nearby tree-tops, chewing on her bottom lip.

"I got your clamp off my brother. We're here to give you a chance to explain before we report you."

"You don't want to do that, Hansen," Jo warned.

"Personally, I hope you don't explain your-self." On *don't*, he went to poke Jo again. Jo was prepared. He grabbed Dec's wrist and held it so firmly that his knuckles turned white. "Let me go," Dec said hoarsely.

"What's your problem, Hansen?" Jo asked. "You're the one got us sent to this backwater rock.

You have no call to come after me about it."

"He thinks you're a traitor, Jo," Lorica explained. "Tell him you're not."

Jo wasn't listening to her, though. He was too mad. "You probably feel right at home here," he said to Dec. "It's all sludge and—and *nothing*. Is this why you joined up, Hansen? To wade through muck and scrap broken-down landspeeders? Couldn't you have just done that back on your bog-trash home planet?"

Dec fumed. He wrenched himself free from Jo's grip, and both of them stumbled back. Jo knocked into AG, sending him sprawling to the ground. AG's landing made a squishing noise that got Sari's attention for a moment before she looked back up to the nearby trees.

"You knock my brother down?" Dec hollered at Jo.

"He didn't mean to!" Lorica shouted.

Dec didn't care. "You try to wipe him? You threaten him? And then you knock him down?" He charged at Jo and dragged him into the mud. They, too, landed with a quaggy sound. It really was a fight now. Sari and Mattis were on the outside of it. Sari was trying to figure out how to get in the middle of it, and whether she wanted to.

She hated to fight. Mattis was distracted by, of all things, a bird circling overhead. It had three dark purple spots on its chest and Mattis felt like it was important in that moment to recall what kind of bird it was. *Typical*, Mattis thought. *Rather than take action, I'm birdwatching. I'm no hero.* He, like Sari, tried to figure out how he could help his friends.

Dec and Jo grappled on the ground, throwing punches and calling each other names through clenched teeth. AG tried to right himself nearby.

"You've had this coming," Jo said, and walloped Dec in the jaw. Dec fell forward onto Jo, elbowing him in the chest, hard.

Lorica threw herself into it. Mattis didn't know what side she was on. It seemed that she was only trying to break up the tussle. She kicked Dec off of Jo. When Dec scrabbled backward, Jo rolled, knocking Lorica into the mud, too. She threw an elbow into the side of his face. And again, Mattis was distracted by that bird, circling slowly, drifting in the air currents. If he could identify what kind of bird it was, he would stop being distracted. Why couldn't he think of it? Why did it seem so important?

Sari was no longer at his side. How long had he been staring into the sky? It was hard to tell

how long anything had been happening. Had the fight lasted seconds? Minutes? Sari was edging around the side of the thatch of brambles on which they fought. She wasn't looking to get into the fight herself, but Mattis could see she desperately wanted to pull someone, anyone, out of the fray.

A few meters from them, Dec and Lorica rolled in the muddy thicket. Jo was pulling Dec off of her. Dec was covered in grime; he probably didn't even know whom he was fighting anymore. Not that that stopped him. Just behind Jo, AG stood, wobbled on his feet, then got knocked down again as Jo backed into him. He made a startled whooping noise.

Oh, no. All at once, Mattis remembered the name of the bird circling them. *The duns thackston.* He prayed all the Phirmist prayers he could remember that he was wrong.

"Sari," Mattis said. "Tell me that's not a duns thackston." Mattis pointed up at the bird, which cawed as if it were greeting the two people looking up at it.

The color drained from Sari's face. "Three purple dots." She looked at the bird then down at the fracas.

"The duns thackston." Mattis swallowed.

No one heard him.

"The duns thackston!" he shouted now. "They build their nests!" Dec, Lorica, and Jo were apart now, panting. But they were focused on each other. "Guys!" At least Lorica looked at him. "They build their nests!"

"What are you talking about, Mattis?" Lorica snarled.

"The duns thackston!"

"What—*oof!*" She was blown over by Dec, who grabbed her and threw her to the ground. "Get off!"

Jo gave Dec a good kick in the side, and as Dec went over, he grabbed on to Jo's leg, pulling him down, too.

"It builds a strong covering of branches and mud and stuff over a sinkhole, you guys!" Mattis tried to warn them, but they really weren't listening. "Sari—get them out."

Sari took a step toward the fighters. Mattis kept trying to explain.

"If there were just a hole in the ground, no animals would . . . They'd go around."

"Shut up about holes, Banz!" Jo barked.

"The duns thackston builds a kind of nest out

of sticks and mud over the hole so that animals will think it's just more ground and walk over it and fall through. They're symbiotic!"

Sari took another step toward them.

"The duns thackston picks clean the bones of whatever they don't finish."

"Of whatever *what* don't finish?" asked Dec.

"Duns thackstons have a symbiotic relationship with sarlaccs!" Mattis shouted, and everybody froze. They were standing above a sarlacc pit? The fight was over.

Sari reached out. "Don't move. Take my hand, Dec."

"I have to move to take your hand," he said, reaching for her. Everyone could feel the ground beneath them giving a little with every shift of weight. The sarlacc's prey tended to be larger than humans, so the nest had lasted so far, but from the sound of it, it wouldn't last much longer.

"Dec, pull Jo with you. You can reach him," Lorica called out.

Dec looked to Jo and then to AG, who had been knocked aside. "Explain yourself, Jo."

Everyone groaned.

"This isn't the time or the place!" Sari yelled.

"Let's get out of danger first and do the rest somewhere else, far, far away."

"Tell us what you're up to, Jo. I got all day," Dec said, reaching out for Jo.

"You smirking *muck-dweller*," Jo yelled, leaping at Dec, tackling him, and pulling Sari onto the thatch, too. The nest cracked and buckled, and as a purple-spotted duns thackston cawed eagerly overhead, Mattis watched his friends crash into the sarlacc pit.

CHAPTER
12

MATTIS GRABBED LORICA'S hand as she fell. The force of it wrenched his shoulder and pulled him to the ground, where he laid at the lip of the pit. He took her other hand and tried to pull her up and out, but to no avail. He started to scoot backward, but he felt his shoulder scream in pain.

"You're not going to be able to pull me out of here," she told him with more calm than he could find in himself.

"Then climb up. Do something!" Mattis panicked.

"There are only teeth under me," she told him, as if that was something he already knew but didn't want to admit. "You have to let me go, Mattis."

"What? No!" he cried.

She kicked at a tentacle grabbing for her foot. The sounds of their friends echoed off the walls.

"Do you hear that?" Lorica asked. "The others are down there fighting for their lives. That means the fall didn't kill them. Now let me go help them fight and buy you the time to save us all."

"How am I going to do that?" Mattis asked.

"By getting us all out of there," she told him matter-of-factly.

"How am I going to do *that?*" Mattis asked, his grip slipping.

"Figure it out!" she yelled as she fell.

A tentacle grabbed her in the air and pulled her out of sight.

Mattis looked around for any sort of rope. A vine would do. Anything that he could lower into the pit and use to pull them out. He scanned the trees. No vines. Plenty of moss. No help. He tossed aside pieces of the duns thackston's remaining nest in case there were any sizable sticks that could reach. Nothing. He wished those speeder bikes had side bags packed with emergency kits for such a situation, and that's when he realized that the answer had been in plain sight the whole time. He climbed onto the speeder bike, pushed it to the edge of the sarlacc pit, and rode it into the humid maw.

Mattis had never wasted an opportunity to go as fast as he was allowed on a speeder bike. He wished they'd trained him for this kind of slow vertical descent. It was more like riding a roto-cropper than a speeder bike, he thought as he realized that he'd performed that action hundreds of times back on Durkteel. Confidence he'd never felt surged through him as he went past the downward-facing teeth that prevented escape. He beamed as he saw his friends, the dregs of J-Squadron, all armed with sticks from the nest, fighting as a team for the first time.

They were standing on soft tissue through which the mostly digested remains of a rancor emerged. A duns thackston picked at the giant creature and cawed angrily at the disturbance.

"Anybody need a ride?" Mattis asked as a tentacle whipped the speeder bike, knocking him onto the ground and covering him with digestive goo. The sarlacc's beaked tongue snatched at Mattis. As it closed around his head, Sari shoved a thick branch into the tender inside of the mandible.

Dec grabbed Mattis by the ankles and pulled him out just as the sarlacc snapped the branch into pieces. "You owe me one, Mattis." Sari winked. "That was my best twig."

She helped Mattis up and he gagged on the rancid breath of the gaping gullet surrounding them. AG gave them sticks to bat the tentacles away and they did.

"I thought the planet stank out there," muttered Mattis.

The sound of the speeder bike powering up drew their attention to Jo and Lorica, who were flying up and out of the pit.

"Just when you think someone has your back, because he literally had your back against this hole-in-the-ground monster, he goes and does a thing like that!" Dec said, taking his frustration out on the sarlacc. "If this thing doesn't kill me, I swear, I'll kill them."

Three tentacles whipped around Dec, and that beaked tongue shot out again. "Sari! Help him!" AG yelled, trying to pull the tentacles off his brother. Sari didn't respond; she couldn't. Tentacles held her tight. Mattis whacked at the tentacles as hard as he could until he felt another one wrap around his foot and flip him upside down. He saw two more pulling at AG, trying to rip him in half. The beaked tongue weaved, pointing to Mattis as if deciding whom to eat first.

It didn't get the chance. Lorica and Jo flew back in on a pair of speeder bikes and dragged their hot engines along the walls of the sarlacc, burning it. The creature bellowed in pain all around them, and its tentacles loosened, then went for Lorica and Jo.

Despite the fear and danger all around them, Mattis felt like they were doing maneuvers they'd practiced a thousand times. Lorica and Jo crisscrossed in the narrow wet space, using a flight pattern that the angry mouth in which they flew couldn't comprehend. Mattis and Dec stood back to back with Sari and AG, turning, defending, reporting status. Lorica and Jo called for the pairs to disengage and separate. Each bike drove between a pair and with a "Now!" familiar from countless evac drills, they mounted the moving speeders and crisscrossed out again. Their momentum shattered the teeth in their path. The bikes took some damage, but not as much as the sarlacc.

The two bikes, with all of J-Squadron cling-ing to them, spit out into the swamp. The speeder bikes shuddered and died. Mattis and his friends fell into a heap, one on top of the other, all of them covered in mud, all of them bloodied and used up, and all of them laughing, just happy to be alive, together.

A crashing noise came from the brush behind them, and though they were drained, all six of them strained to their feet and took a defensive position. Where one ended and the next began must have been difficult to discern, so caked in mud and sticks and gunk were they. Which explained why, as he burst out of the brush on his speeder bike, Klimo cried out in horror.

Seeing it was them, he said, "Friends! What did I miss?"

CHAPTER

13

B Y EVENING, they'd traded the mud- and gloop-crusted clothing for clean jumpsuits that they found on the transport shuttles. Those got fairly muck-covered, too—that was inevitable on Vodran—but at least there was no sarlacc goo on them.

While the rest of them were falling into and climbing out of the sarlacc pit, Klimo had stumbled onto a small ridge. It was circled by creeping vegetation and shrouded by low-slung treetops, but its center was clear and somewhat dry. There they built a fire. They'd regret bringing piles of blankets out to the ridge, but the thought of sleeping in the transports reminded them too much of the claustrophobia of being inside the sarlacc's mouth. Plus, Dec snored. Out there, his sleep snorts would be just one instrument in the orchestra of animal noises surrounding them all night.

They ate double rations. Dec told them there were enough varmints in the swamps that, with him around, they could survive for months. Thanks to the group, he added, he was around.

They did their best to find dry wood and piled it onto the fire. They burned their ration wrappings. The sky—the sun had been veiled behind cloud cover all day—went from a light gray to a dark gray to a painted bluish purple. They sat on blankets in a circle, full, exhausted, and alive.

"This is a good squadron, you guys!" Klimo's enthusiasm hadn't waned, but he wasn't bouncing around the clearing. His body was as spent as everyone else's. Hiking through the bogs and scavenging odd scraps had done him in. "J-Squadron could take down the First Order all by ourselves!"

They all laughed, except for Jo. "We're getting there," he said, which seemed an enormous concession to the rest of them. "We'll make pilots of you. I'm sure of it."

Dec shook his head. "We *are* pilots, man.

Doesn't it make any difference what happened here today?"

Jo held Dec's gaze. There was no malice in it, as there might have been just that morning.

"Why do you want to fly?" Jo asked him.

"I already fly," Dec replied. "In my head, I'm in the clouds."

"Your head is definitely in the clouds," Lorica said snarkily. She was back to her irritable self, but there was a good-naturedness to it.

"I'm serious," Dec said. "Aygee and me—you said it before. We're swamp rats. We been down in the muck so long there's mud in our lungs. And that ain't a complaint. I like where I'm from. I like our people. I love 'em. But there were nights when Aygee and me would lay on the roof of our home and look up at them stars. . . . There's a world out there. I'm good enough to do good in it. I already helped all I could on Ques, fixin' folks' vehicles and the like. I reckoned it was time for me to fix bigger things. Flyin' is a way to do that."

They were all silent a moment. Each of them owned a version of Dec's recital. Mattis thought, *If we ask Jo his version, maybe the truth will come out.* After Jo's heroic turn at the sarlacc pit, Mattis couldn't believe he was a traitor. Then, of course, Mattis was clever enough to know that letting his entire squad die was no way for Jo to work his way up the Resistance ranks. Which left Jo with what loyalty?

"I felt the same," Mattis said. "Except, I can't fix things and people tend not to like me."

They laughed, and AG said, "That ain't true."

Mattis shook his head. "I don't mean they dislike me. I just mean they don't think of me. I'm Mattis." He remembered Klimo's words. "I'm just another person. Just another speck on a planet in a system of planets in a galaxy . . . I think I can fly, though. I love to do it, but I've only ever done it a couple meters off the ground on the farm or in deep space in my dreams. Or in the sims, I guess, but that's never leaving the ground. When I believe in something, I'm pretty sure I can do it. And I believe I will be the greatest pilot anyone's ever seen." They laughed again, and he laughed with them. What Mattis didn't add was: *I have the Force. It flows through me.*

He hadn't meant to speak so much, but now that he had, he seemed unable to stop. And they didn't want him to. No one had ever listened to Mattis that much. He felt both safe and utterly exposed. "I want to make a difference," he said.

"Before I joined the Resistance, I didn't know about the First Order, but I knew there was bad in the universe. There was bad in the orphanage where I grew up. So there must be bigger bad across the galaxy. I don't want bad things to happen to good people. So. Here I am. Learning to fly. Fighting against the bad people to help the good ones."

He was out of breath. He took shallow gulps, trying to hide it. He wished someone else would talk. Maybe the Force was working after all, because Lorica spoke.

"I didn't do the things people say I did."

An invisible wave ruffled all of them. They couldn't help it. Lorica's words were surprising and discouraging. She dropped her forehead into her hands, then lowered her palms onto her knees and sat up straight. "I've never told anyone," she said.

"You're talking about the weapons cache?" Sari said. "It belonged to smugglers. You blew it up."

"It blew up, that's true," Lorica said. "I was just . . . there. My parents own a luxury hotel on Kergans in the New Republic. This was a couple of years ago. I was in a very expensive school. I learned to hunt with bassa hounds. I learned to ride fathiers in competition. I hated all of it. What I liked was flying. They bought me a brand-new SoroSuub Petite Opu-Yacht. It was gold, of course. Everyone at the Academy envied it. And I loved it, but not for the reasons they did, because of the way it looked or because it was expensive. I loved it because it meant I could go anywhere I wanted to go. That ship was freedom. I flew from one end of Kergans to the other. The planet wasn't big enough for me.

"I was also reckless. As much as the ship meant to me, I didn't take care of it. I scratched it up on the sides of structures and bridges. There are a lot of bridges on Kergans. It was full of dents and divots after just a week. It didn't matter. My parents would have it repaired.

"I left it outside the hotel one afternoon. I was only stopping in for a moment for food and to spend some credits. The yacht hovered at the entrance, gleaming, beautiful. A light freighter came screaming into our landing strip and smashed right through it, exploding both ships. It's a good thing my ship was there or the freighter might have gone right through the front of my parents' hotel. I was only steps from the landing strip. If I were slower, I'd have blown up, too.

"We didn't know what that freighter was or what its pilot was trying to do. The Kergans Security Force found the illegal weapons on board the remains of the freighter. They were the first ones to congratulate me on my work for the New Republic. Then people started talking. I was a hero. I'd saved the hotel, the city, Kergans, the Republic. What could I say? Should I have told them it was an accident?

"So," Lorica finished. "That's why I fly. I'm already getting credit for being a hero. I thought I should make myself one for real."

Mattis didn't waste any time telling her, "You will. I'm sure of it." As he said it, he realized he *was* sure. Lorica, despite her jagged personality, was a good person.

"Lotta secrets comin' out, eh?" AG intoned. He was pointedly looking at Jo.

"Here's another," Jo said. They all leaned in, despite not wanting to betray their interest. "Lorica tried to talk me out of erasing your memory, Aygee-Ninety." He let them chew on that a moment. "That's why she was there at droid maintenance that night. She told me you're a good pilot. That it's your glitches that make you one. Mind you, I was mad enough that I wasn't minding what she was saying, but what she was saying was sound. A reasonable argument. I think your glitches *could* make you a great pilot. It's possible. The enemy could never predict your actions."

He looked around the group, meeting the eyes of each member. "That's true of all of you. I tried to make you all pilots by the book. It's what made sense to me. But I discounted what each of you brings to the table. You're all full of glitches," he said. They laughed.

"More than most," Dec agreed.

"And it's those glitches that make you all what you are. And it's what makes you all great. And that's why the First Order will never defeat us."

"Since you brought it up . . ." Dec began.

"I'm not a traitor," Jo said. He watched the fire, wouldn't meet anyone's gaze. "But my parents are First Order officers."

Jo laughed at their collective gasp, which broke the tension. "They're . . . good parents, is what's strange. They're just *so wrong* about the First Order. They think it will make the galaxy better, but the things they talk about . . . It won't. The First Order is bad. We have to defeat it."

Sari asked, "But—they can't know you've joined

the Resistance, right? That would be—that would be—" She didn't have words for it. *Confusing* was one, but that didn't begin to cover it.

"They don't. They think I'm at the New Republic Military Academy on Ganthel. But the commander at that academy is sympathetic to the Resistance. She sent me here, and she covers for me. General Organa knows; so does Admiral Ackbar. They allow me to talk with my parents. *That*," he said to AG, "is what you saw the night you spied on me."

Mattis was so relieved, he nearly started crying.

Klimo, on the other hand, bawled like a baby. "That must be so ha-ha-harrrrd!" Sari rubbed his back gently.

AG nodded. "I'm sorry," he said.

They all mumbled apologies to Jo, then sat for a moment in an abundant silence, broken only by Klimo's snorfling.

"I fly because I like math," Sari said.

She didn't get a chance to explain further, because that was when a panicked, bleating tauntaun crashed through their campsite.

CHAPTER
14

"THAT WAS A TAUNTAUN," Klimo observed a moment after the animal had run bleating back into the brush. The tauntaun had blown over the ridge, knocking flaming logs from their campsite. The logs sizzled on the soggy ground.

They all stood, looking around, waiting for an explanation, maybe wondering whether that tauntaun had been a collective dream, because Vodran was the farthest planet from the animal's native icy Hoth in every way.

Sari took a few steps toward the brush where the large animal had disappeared. "Why would a tauntaun—"

They heard the stampede before they saw it. The bleating of tauntauns—more than one—but other animals, too. Roars and grunts and howls. And they were getting louder.

"Run!" Mattis yelled, but it wasn't soon enough. The animals were upon them. Three tauntauns leaped over the ridge, crashing through and caroming off of Sari, who fell backward into the muck. The herd kicked up a flock of long-necked, speckled swamp birds that screeched as they took wing. Lorica tackled Mattis and threw him off the ridge and into the bog as the other animals bounded through. A pair of clawed, toothy, slinky nexu, gnashing at the fleeing tauntauns and whatever else went near them, didn't stop to attack. They, too, ran with the herd. They, too, did not belong on the planet.

Mattis peered over the ridge as more and more animals galloped through. A heavy-hoofed bassa hound nearly took off Mattis's head. Luckily, Mattis jerked back and all he received was a faceful of mud. Wiping it away, he saw Klimo across the ridge, jumping into some underbrush. Or at least, Klimo attempted to jump into some underbrush. Instead, he took a flying leap and was met midair by a lumbering moof. Klimo bounced against the animal's thick hide, then dropped back down into the mud. For once, the Rodian didn't come up short and rolled away in time for the moof's hoof to barely miss him. Lorica yanked Mattis back below the ridge before he could locate any more of their friends.

"We have to help them," he yelled over the cacophony of footfalls, bellows, and yawps.

"When this passes," Lorica hissed.

"When this passes it'll be too late!" Mattis snapped back. He went to rise, and Lorica pulled him down again.

Then, clearly thinking better of his idea, she said, "Okay," and hoisted him up onto the ridge. They were in the middle of the stampede. Animals surged around them like water around jutting rocks. If they were still, they got nudged side to side by a passing jefflac or bumbling dewback that hardly noticed them at all. Something else had the animals' attention: escape. They were all running from something.

Whatever it was surely was coming, which meant Mattis and Lorica had little time to help their friends. Quickly scanning the ridge, Mattis found Sari and Klimo. The Rodian had made it to the underbrush and was doing his best to stay hidden and safe. Good. Mattis just hoped Klimo didn't get stomped by something bigger than the pack of moss lenas that were bolting through his hiding space.

Sari, however, was in more dire circumstances. Her back was to them, but Mattis could tell she was defending herself against something large. She took rapid but tentative swings with her fists against whatever she was blocking from their view. Mattis pointed, and as quickly as they were able, he and Lorica made their way to her.

Sari was fighting a ginzy. The creature was about half Sari's size, but it was thick, with chunky clay-colored and blond feathers. Its tiny hands ended in hooked talons. The ginzy stood on two skinny legs and swiped at Sari with its talons. Behind the creature, Dec was hunched in the mud, clutching his side. The ginzy made a nonstop, atonal gibbering noise to distract its enemies.

"How's it going?" Lorica asked, dodging a ginzy talon lash.

"It tore a chunk out of Dec," Sari said. "We have to get him out of here. Something is coming."

Mattis nodded curtly. "You two can handle it." Lorica shot him a withering look. "I would die!"

It shouldn't have made Lorica and Sari laugh, but it did. "Get Dec," Lorica said.

Mattis circled the ginzy, and the creature followed him with its black eyes. As if they'd practiced it for years, Sari and Lorica leaped at the ginzy, each grabbing one of its feathered arms. The ginzy shrieked and gibbered, but neither girl let go. They held its wrists so it couldn't slash them.

Mattis rolled Dec over and saw the long slice the ginzy had left in his friend's side. "Can you walk?"

"Do I haveta?" Dec moaned.

The stampede grew thinner, with just a few small or overly large animals. They heard a rumble and crunch of branches as something big moved toward them through the swamp.

"Yes," Mattis said. They stood, Mattis supporting Dec as they stumbled away from the ridge.

"Meet us at the transports!" Lorica shouted as they ran.

Mattis helped Dec get back to the transport ships. He left Dec on the boarding ramp of one. "Get this running," he said. "I'll be back with the others. We have to get out of here."

Mattis didn't wait for Dec to protest, just bolted back the way they had come, slogging through the bog until he was back at that ridge. It was dark, and he could barely make out the path. But their fire still lit the clearing. That was how Mattis saw the tawd swarm approaching.

Tawds were vile, bile-dripping animals of a sort one might get if a wampa mated with a rathtar. All teeth and mucus and fur. Usually snow-white, these tawds—there were six of them—were caked with swamp muck. They bowled toward the ridge, mewling and growling. One tawd could destroy a dozen farms by eating every living thing and destroying what remained. Six would surely end them all.

The two tawds in the lead of the swarm bounded up the ridge, heading directly for Sari and Lorica, who still held the snapping, pulling ginzy between them. Pink bile flung from a tawd's jaws into the fire and sent sparks spitting out.

Mattis heard Lorica grunt, "Throw!" as the tawds barreled toward them. She and Sari pushed the ginzy into the two oncoming tawds, one of which barely stopped to snatch the taloned monkey-thing in its teeth. The other tawd, seeing the ginzy's kicking feet, chomped down on them. Together, they pulled the ginzy apart.

The other four tawds smashed into the two already on the ridge. Seeing Lorica and Sari, all six hunched on their short front legs, fanning out their spiked tails. This was a sign of imminent attack.

"Hey!" Mattis shouted. "Over here! Look at me!"

The tawds turned as one, bellow-growled, and pounced. He was just far enough away that they missed, and he didn't look back to find out how small the gap between them was. He pushed through the bog back toward the ships, the tawds making slick chomping noises behind him. Out of the corner of his eye he saw Sari and Lorica running along with him. If they could make the ships, they'd be safe. Tawds were vicious, but they weren't large. And he thought—if AG had made it back—that they could get out of there before the swarm dismantled the transports.

He hoped AG had made it back, and Jo, as well. He worried that he hadn't seen them or Klimo since the stampede. He worried they might be lost forever on Vodran. He also worried he might be eaten by those tawds, but somehow that immediate fear seemed insignificant. The Force was with him. It would keep him safe.

He came into the clearing with the tawd

swarm behind him. Sari plowed into a tawd just as it lunged for Mattis's head. She knocked it off course, but in righting herself, she pushed Mattis into the mud and in the way of another drooling tawd. It bore down on him and, thinking quickly, Mattis rolled through the mud into an overturned log. He heard the tawd chewing on the thick bark, but that would slow it down. Thank the Force. He was safe for now.

Mattis listened, trying to figure out whether everyone else was safe. He heard a boarding ramp raise. That must mean Sari and Lorica had successfully boarded the transport Dec was manning. Maybe the others, too. He was listening so intently to those distant sounds that Mattis didn't notice when the tawd stopped gnawing on his protective trunk. That was odd. He'd have thought it would have gone until it broke through, at which time Mattis would have raced for the other transport. So where was the tawd?

Mattis dared to crawl through the hollowed-out trunk to peer out the other end. The tawds were rolling and pouncing away, retreating back into the swamp. Why had they given up?

As he crawled out of the overturned trunk, Mattis got his answer: rancors.

CHAPTER

15

FOUR OF THEM circled the transports. Each was twice the size of their ships, if not bigger. They had jagged rows of teeth with meat still stuck in them and long, branch-like fingers ending in blade-sharp claws. One was feeding itself the remains of one of the tawds; chunks of the dead animal dropped into the mud below.

The rancors sniffed the clearing with their snubby snouts and grunted, hunting. They knew prey was nearby. Mattis froze. Of course. Rancors. Vodran had belonged to Harra the Hutt, Mattis recalled. Admiral Ackbar had told them all about it. Harra made her fortune buying, selling, and trading exotic animals to other Hutts around the galaxy. When Harra the Hutt had abandoned the planet, it was assumed she'd taken her business with her. It seemed that she hadn't and that her animals had returned to the wild, thriving even in that harsh environment. The rancors, and the other animals, too, were left to roam free. Left to hunt.

One of the rancors spotted Mattis and growled deeply. The others all turned toward him. That low rumbling grew louder, angrier. The rancor that had first noticed Mattis took a lumbering step forward, reaching out its long arm. Mattis dove behind the fallen tree. The rancor lifted it up and tossed it aside as if it were a stick. It advanced on Mattis until a second rancor pushed it aside.

The rancors snapped and growled at each other, fighting over their easy prey. Finally, one of them snatched for him again, just as the boarding ramp to Dec's transport opened with a sharp hiss. The rancor pack turned as one and made for the ship immediately.

Mattis rolled back into the mud and nearby brush. He was shaking, his whole body racked with fear. His teeth banged together; his head sounded like a rockslide. His shoulders, though he lay in the mud, were hot with terror. He peered out from the brush, but he could barely take in the scene without making himself sick.

The rancors surrounded Dec's transport as it lifted out of the mud. Dec and Lorica hung on the ramp, firing the little stun rods they'd been given for defense against dianogas (which they had, stupidly, left on the ships earlier). The flares had little effect on the rancors, who swatted at the hovering ship. Sari did well steering just out of the rancors' reach. She made sure all four were interested, which they very much were, and jetted forward a bit. The rancors followed her. At that rate, she could distract them long enough for Mattis to get on board the other ship with Klimo.

Klimo! He'd made it to the other transport. He sat in the cockpit, waving madly for Mattis to join him. Mattis leaped to his feet. If he made it to Klimo's ship, they could take off and find AG and Jo. The others could get free.

Klimo was behind the controls of the transport. He pumped his fist at the other ship and punched the controls. His ship hovered in the air, distracting the rancors from Dec's transport. What was he doing? Their plan, spontaneous as it was, had been working!

Mattis was in the middle of the clearing when two of the rancors lost interest in Dec's ship. He suddenly found himself between them. They roared at each other. One grabbed for Mattis, and the other batted the first rancor's claws away. A close call for Mattis and a lucky one. He wouldn't be that lucky again. He dove into the knee-deep bog water and tried to keep out of sight. Both rancors splashed around, scraping in the mud with those scythe-like claws, looking for him, roaring.

The other two rancors were attacking the ships. One walloped Klimo's ship, sending it spinning into Dec's. Dec held on then climbed back into the transport, but Lorica was launched into the muck below.

It was chaos as Lorica evaded one rancor, Mattis two more, and Klimo's ship went plunging into the swamp. If Mattis and Lorica didn't get to it, they'd be eaten for sure.

Rancors lunged again for Dec's ship, and it rose higher to dodge them.

Mattis and Lorica crawled for Klimo's ship. A rancor claw came down close to Mattis. He rolled. Lucky again. That luck couldn't hold.

Klimo gunned his transport out of the mud. None of the animals was paying him much attention, which was lucky, too. That might be their chance, but there were rancors between them and the ship.

Dec's transport dipped again, then buzzed around the clearing. It was hard to maneuver in so small a space, but Sari was doing it. Her math, Mattis thought, wasn't failing her. Distracted, the rancors chased her, waving their long arms in the air, clawing at the ship and sometimes scratching and denting it. But she kept on until, finally, Mattis and Lorica dragged themselves onto the boarding ramp of Klimo's vessel.

"Friends!" Klimo said. "You made it!"

"We made it, friend," Mattis agreed. "Now let's get out of here."

Mattis rolled over and gave a thumbs-up to the other ship. He could see Dec in the cockpit, grinning but determined. He could see Sari beside him, keeping the transport aloft in odd loops and corners. Dec nodded, turned, and said something to Sari, and suddenly the transport ship blasted into the night sky. It was only moments until it was indistinguishable from the stars beyond.

One ship gone, the rancors turned toward the other. The beasts were smarter than Mattis had realized. They hadn't forgotten. They were also faster than he'd realized. All four galloped toward the ship. Klimo punched the controls, and the ship lifted into the air. Mattis and Lorica were still on the boarding ramp when a rancor—the biggest and tallest of the pack—grabbed on to it. Its claws sunk into the metal of the ship. The rancor roared. It tore the boarding ramp off, throwing Mattis and Lorica back into the bog. Mattis landed hard, the wind knocked out of his lungs. He heard Lorica beside him, saw her in a fog as she dragged herself into a crouch and then kicked him back to reality.

"Move," she breathed. They did. They limped and struggled out of the fray while the rancors were still distracted by Klimo's ship. The largest of the rancors hadn't let the ship go. With all of its weight, it hauled the ship from the sky and smashed it into the swamp, splitting the vessel open like a nut. In a moment, all four rancors were upon it, clawing at the metal and rending the transport.

Mattis tried to get to it, to save Klimo, but Lorica held him back. There was nothing he could do. If Mattis made for the ship, threw himself in the middle of the wild rancors, he'd be dead, too.

Klimo was gone. Their friend, always so enthusiastic, always so happy, was gone. But they would be next if they didn't move out of there.

Lorica hadn't taken two steps, practically dragging Mattis along with her, when the rancors turned again to find them. All four rose from their hunched positions over the remains of the second transport ship. The rancors moved toward them. There was no reason to rush their quarry any longer. Mattis and Lorica were trapped. There was no escape. Lorica took Mattis's hand. They faced the rancors.

"Y'all lovebirds mind if we butt in?" AG's voice came from the wall of twisted trees behind them.

Without thinking, both Mattis and Lorica plunged into the copse from which they'd heard AG's voice. The rancors were quick behind them, picking up and throwing the trees, smashing them into splinters, crushing them into the mud under their wide feet. But Mattis and Lorica stayed a step ahead, finally stumbling into a clearing where AG and Jo had their ramshackle speeder bikes.

"Climb on," Jo commanded. Mattis was happy

to follow orders. He climbed onto one bike behind AG while Lorica leaped onto the other behind Jo.

"Hang on," AG said, and as the rancors crashed after them, both gunned the speeder bikes, whizzing around and past the creatures and leaving the rancors to lumber behind, never fast enough to catch up.

CHAPTER
16

THEY SPED THROUGH the swamps until the complaining roars of the rancors could no longer be heard. Then they raced even farther. They didn't stop until the trees had thinned and the land beneath them was more meadow than bog. A distant sun lightened the sky north of them. Finally, they were safe.

When they stopped, they compared their stories. Jo asked, "Klimo?" and Mattis shook his head. Jo bowed his own head. They were all exhausted; even AG seemed wiped out from the efforts of the past couple of days. Jo surprised them by saying that he thought Klimo would have been good for the squadron.

"He wasn't just a funny, weird little scrontch farmer," Jo said. "He really wanted to make a difference."

"Well, he *was* a funny, weird little scrontch farmer," AG added with a smirk in his voice.

"Yeah, but not *just*," said Lorica.

"I don't think we would've gotten away with—" Mattis wanted to say "Klimo's sacrifice," but he couldn't make his mouth form the words. He sobbed into his hands. Things were as bad as they could ever get.

"Where will Dec and Sari go?" Lorica asked. "We don't know where the base is. The cargo ship won't return for weeks, and they can't just fly in circles until then."

"They'll come back for us," Mattis said.

Lorica shook her head. "When they see what's left of the second ship, they'll think we're dead. And then they'll leave again."

"They'll look for us," AG said. "We're their friends. We're their people."

"How will they find us?" Mattis asked. His head hurt, his body hurt; he didn't want to think of details. He wanted to sleep. He wanted to be somewhere safe, in a bed.

"We'll make sure they can," AG said. "We'll make ourselves conspicuous."

"At least we can get around," Jo added, smiling at the bikes. Mattis couldn't imagine smiling. Not for a long time.

AG noticed. "Look," he said. He took Mattis by the shoulders. The four of them stood in a small square. "We're safe. We got away. We're alive. We faced more in the past couple a days than any of us have ever seen before, and we survived. Together. And that's what we're gonna do from here on out."

Mattis nodded. Then, as it occurred to him, he actually did smile. "Besides," he said. "How could things get worse?"

"All of you, freeze where you are." The voice came from behind Mattis, but as he heard it, he saw the armor-clad figures coming into view all around them. They had weapons. They surrounded Mattis and his friends. By the insignia on their armor, he knew what they were.

First Order stormtroopers.

Things had just gotten worse.

Acker & Blacker wish to thank Michael Siglain for the opportunity, Jen Heddle for being the strongest and gentlest of editors, and Annie Wu for the beautiful, inspiring art. Thanks to Julie Lacouture for patience and early reads. And thanks to all of you Adventurekateers for your constant enthusiasm. *Clink.*

BEN ACKER & BEN BLACKER are the creators and writers/producers of the *Thrilling Adventure Hour*, a staged show in the style of old-time radio that is also a podcast on the Nerdist network. In television, they have written for CW's *Supernatural*, Dreamworks/Netflix's *Puss in Boots*, and FX's *Cassius and Clay*. They've also developed original pilots for Fox, USA (twice), Spike, Paramount, Nickelodeon, and other entities. In comics, they've written for Marvel, Dynamite, Boom!, and others.

Acker has written for PRI's *Wits*.

Blacker is the creator and host of *The Writers Panel*, a podcast about the business and process of writing, as well as its spin-off, the *Nerdist Comics Panel*. He's the producer of *Dead Pilots Society*, a podcast in which unproduced television pilots by established writers are given the table reads they so richly deserve.

ANNIE WU is an illustrator currently living in Chicago. She is best known for her work in comics, including DC's *Black Canary* and Marvel's *Hawkeye*.

Jabari

J.B Happyfeet